# ADAM

## RIDING HARD
## BOOK 1

# JENNIFER
# ASHLEY

# Chapter One

Adam heard himself flatline. The machine shrilled one long sound, and everything he'd ever known vanished. He saw no light, felt nothing; he had no body, did not exist.

There had been a roar, red fire, the stunt crew yelling, his best friend trapped in a pickup, surrounded by flame, eyes fixed in an unseeing stare. Then paramedics, fire trucks, noise, smoke, something jammed to Adam's face. And then nothing except lying motionless while the machine sang out that Adam Campbell was dead.

Next to his bed, a woman was crying. Couldn't be his mother; she never cried when things were bad. She'd get through it and then go to pieces later, like she'd done when his dad had died.

Dad had been about thirty-two when he'd passed—Adam was four years younger than that. *Sorry, Dad, meant to take care of them a little longer.*

Bright, hot fire blasted through Adam's body, streaking along every nerve. Adam's legs jerked, his fingers burned, pain seared through his chest to shoot upwards into his brain. *What the f—?*

He slammed back down on the bed, gasping for air. Cold and dry, it grated into his lungs. The machines stopped their long scream and started a rhythm, soft signals that overlapped one another and pulsed like his heart.

*Beat* ... pause ... *beat* ... pause ...

A very long time later, Adam peeled open his eyes.

They surrounded his bed, his mom flanked by four big, tough-looking men—Tyler, Grant, Ross, and Carter. Carter's large hand rested on the shoulder of his eight-year-old daughter, Faith's hazel eyes enormous in her small face.

His family had come all the way from Riverbend to watch him die.

"Hey," Adam croaked. His throat was raw with serious pain, his voice barely audible. "I feel like shit."

His younger brothers, Faith, and his mother relaxed into wide smiles—except for Carter, who'd never caught on to what smiling was all about. But even Carter's eyes warmed, the hand on Faith's shoulder easing.

For some reason, they were all very, very happy with Adam.

# Chapter Two

Bailey watched the family drive in. She remained in the big corral, with Dodie on the other end of the longe line, teaching the horse to master her latest tricks for the upcoming movie shoot.

"You're supposed to be afraid," Bailey told the chocolate-brown horse waiting patiently for her cue. "Not enjoying it. No one's going to buy that."

Dodie reared up when Bailey gave the signal, pawing the air, then came down and danced aside, shuddering. Perfect shot—that should have been a take—but Dodie looked, well, *smug*. Bailey refused to actually scare a horse to make the trick work—no one on the Circle C Ranch was cruel to horses—so this was the best it was going to get. If the camera caught Dodie's movements and edited out that the mare was overacting, it should work.

A black SUV and two pickups rolled to the house on the rise, the family climbing out. Bailey moved to the rail to watch.

The entire Campbell family had flown to L.A. when word had come that Adam had been pulled out of the burning wreckage of a movie stunt gone wrong, barely alive. He was an experienced stuntman, but Adam performed some of the most dangerous feats in the business, and accidents happened.

Adam's mom had stayed out there with him for a few weeks while he began his healing, his brothers going back and forth, but they'd all congregated today to bring him home from the airport in Austin.

Bailey's heart had dropped like a stone when she'd heard about Adam's accident. Olivia Campbell, Adam's mother and Bailey's current employer, had asked Bailey if she'd like to come with them, knowing Baily and Adam had once been close. Bailey had declined, though it had taken all her resolve to not rush to his bedside. She knew the family would want to be together if they lost him, no outsiders.

Whether Adam made it or not, Bailey didn't trust herself not to betray her feelings. She and Adam had led very different lives since age eighteen, when they'd both left the small town of Riverbend, Texas, to go their separate ways—he to Hollywood to wrangle horses and ride in movies; Bailey to Austin and UT.

They'd parted as friends, each moving on to other relationships, but when Bailey had heard the news that Adam might not survive, she'd realized that, in her heart, it had always been Adam.

Bailey stilled as she caught sight of Adam in the passenger seat. The longe line went slack, and Dodie joined Bailey at the fence, the horse watching with her.

Adam was helped out of the truck by Grant on one side, Carter on the other. Small Faith moved like a satellite between them, her hands out as though ready to catch her uncle Adam in case he slipped.

Bailey saw Adam make a curt gesture at his brothers as he adjusted his crutches. She could guess what he was saying: *Don't baby me. I'm older than you.*

Dodie, recognizing the family, let out a throaty neigh of welcome.

Every single one of them turned and looked down to the corrals. Tyler and Grant waved, and Bailey lifted her hand in return.

Faith made a gesture to Adam, as though telling him not to fall while she was gone, and broke away toward Bailey. She pranced to the corral in her imitation of a horse's canter, and Dodie's ears pricked.

Now Adam was looking down the slope. He raised a hand to shade his eyes. *Who is that?* he'd be asking.

One of his brothers, probably Grant, the second-oldest Campbell, would answer. *Your ex. She works for us now.*

Grant liked to teasingly call Bailey "Adam's Ex." A year younger than Adam, Grant had been a good friend the few weeks Bailey and Adam had gone out.

At the time, Bailey had kept Adam from flunking out of school by helping him through the last of his exams so he could stand up and graduate with his class. They'd had a small, intense fling—the kind you have when you're young and poised on the edge of adulthood—then they'd gone their separate ways.

No recriminations, no hurting. They'd both been ready to get on with their lives.

*Who am I kidding?* Bailey had told herself, when Adam was offered the chance to take his riding skills to Hollywood, that her rosy dreams of marrying him and settling down had been just that, dreams. Not reality.

Bailey had accepted a scholarship to the University of Texas in Austin and started her own life, quickly earning a bachelor's then a master's degree in math and computer science, working as a programmer in a large tech company after that. Interesting projects, long hours, lots of money, a new kind of crowd, a three-year marriage, and a divorce.

When she'd discovered the true nature of her cheating husband, and the lack of loyalty among their friends, she'd quit her antacid-popping job and returned to her roots in the little town of Riverbend, in the heart of Hill Country. She'd asked Olivia Campbell and her sons, the best stunt trainers in the business, for a job. Bailey might be a math geek, but she'd grown up with horses and knew how to bring out the best in them.

The Campbells, along with their foster brother, Carter Sullivan, were stunt riders and horse trainers, their talents highly sought after, their acts popular at rodeos and exhibitions throughout Texas. Adam had been snatched up to work full-time on movies by California studios, while the other brothers were wranglers and horse stunt riders for small-studio movies, television, and commercials throughout Texas and New Mexico.

Bailey knew when she came home that she didn't want to work anywhere else. Her stress levels had gone way down in the last year—she'd arrived burned out and defeated, and now she slept like a baby. The Campbells had offered Bailey a refuge, and she'd taken it.

And now Adam was home.

The brothers were pretending not to hover around him, but they surrounded Adam like bodyguards as he hobbled onto the porch and finally dropped into a waiting chair. The crutches that had held him up clattered to the wooden porch floor.

Adam irritably waved off his brothers as they stooped to retrieve the crutches, and again, Bailey imagined what he was saying: *Stop fussing and grab me a beer.*

Bailey saw Olivia shake her head and Adam flop his hands to the arms of the chair in resignation. Probably he couldn't have any alcohol on whatever meds he was on.

Olivia would offer him her famous iced tea now — not sweet tea, which Adam didn't like. Adam gave a nod, and Olivia walked into the house.

From this angle, Bailey could see through the window into the living room. Olivia was heading to the kitchen, wiping her eyes.

Faith reached the corral. She was horse-wise enough to stop fluttering around once near Dodie, but she was still excited.

Faith addressed Dodie first. "I don't have any treats for you," she said as the mare lowered her nose to Faith's hands. "But if you're good, I'll sneak you some tortilla chips later. You know she really likes those," Faith said to Bailey.

Six months ago, when Dodie'd had the horse equivalent of a bad cold, the only things she would eat were tortilla chips and pizza. Faith was convinced they'd saved her life.

"Uncle Adam growled all the way from Austin," Faith said. "He growled on the plane from L.A. too. He is *not* a good patient, Grandma says."

"Can't blame him." Bailey observed the brothers trying to make their oldest sibling comfortable. "The wreck was really bad."

"A truck crashed into his motorcycle then Uncle Adam and the truck smashed into a building that fell down on them, and the pickup blew up. For real. The other stuntman died, and Uncle Adam is really upset about it. He doesn't say that, but we can tell."

Bailey had heard details of the accident from Olivia and Grant, but Faith's matter-of-fact summation made her heart constrict. "It's terrible. I'm so sorry."

"Uncle Adam broke a lot of bones, and his face is all burned, but his injuries weren't as bad as they could have been, the doctors told us. Uncle Adam's mad—not that he was hurt, but that nothing more happened to him. He keeps saying *Dawson died, and all I got was a broken leg and a sissy burn.*"

Bailey's hand tightened on the longe line until her knuckles hurt. "Poor Adam."

Adam Campbell didn't like to show his emotions. He'd be gruff and growling, all the while his heart was breaking. Bailey had seen that in him before, and she didn't like that it was happening again.

"We feel bad for him," Faith said, in her clear-eyed way. "But he doesn't want us feeling bad, so that makes him angry too. It's complicated, Dad says."

Faith's dad was Carter Sullivan, whose life had been extremely complicated before Olivia had brought him here to foster him.

"I guess we have to let him heal," Bailey said. She leaned her arms on the top rail of the corral and gazed at Adam on the porch, surrounded by tall Campbell men.

Dodie stretched her neck down to Faith again, so Faith could keep petting her. All the horses liked Faith, except for Buster, but he was a crabby old fart who hated everybody.

"I guess," Faith said. "Grandma says, do you want to stay for dinner?"

Up at the house, the brothers were dropping away from Adam, one by one, to unload the SUV, to go inside and help Olivia, or head to the barn to help settle the horses for the night. Adam remained in the chair, alone, giving Bailey a clear view of him.

He sat there, exhausted, broken, and Bailey's heart squeezed again. Adam had always been so *alive*. Being with him had been like holding a lit firework. He'd had a restless energy that could fuel a rocket, and a smile that lit up the sky.

Now he sat, head back, body still. Adam Campbell never, ever sat still.

As though he sensed her, Adam raised his head and looked down the hill.

Bailey could feel his intense blue gaze, those eyes framed with the blackest lashes she'd ever seen. His hair wasn't black, it was dark brown—when they'd been kids, it had always been burned with blond streaks. These days he wore it short, and the streaks weren't as obvious, but the short cut revealed every line of his handsome face.

Now that face was burned and scarred, she'd heard from Grant, though she couldn't see it from here. Beautiful Adam used to have every girl in town quivering when he walked by. Even ones who considered themselves too sophisticated for a local cowboy had turned their heads to watch him pass. They'd made sure their breasts turned in his direction too, and Adam hadn't been oblivious.

Bailey had gone a lot further with him than those girls ever dreamed — but that was a long time ago.

"Not sure it's a good idea," Bailey said in answer to Faith's offer of supper. "I don't want to make Adam self-conscious."

"Oh, come on, Bailey, *pleeeze*? He'll want to see you. I know all about you and Adam in the old days — Dad told me. Adam's still in love with you."

Bailey looked at her in alarm. "Adam told you that, did he?"

"He doesn't have to tell me," Faith said, stroking Dodie's neck. "I *know*."

Sweet of her, but Bailey wasn't stupid. There had been too many years, too many differences in their lives, to think anything she'd kindled with Adam in high school would remain. He'd recover from his injuries and return to Hollywood, and Bailey would stay here, working with the Campbells, enjoying the unhurried pace of her life.

That was how it would be.

"Okay, Bailey?" Faith said. "You're staying, right?"

Bailey sighed as she unhooked the longe line from Dodie and started winding it up. She'd have to face Adam sometime, and it might as well be now as later. They'd get the awkwardness out of the way then go on with their lives until he left again.

"All right," she told Faith. "Help me put away Dodie, and I'll stay for dinner."

"Woot!" Faith climbed through the bars and easily caught sweet-tempered Dodie by the halter. Bailey snapped on the lead rope, and Faith happily led Dodie to her stall as the sun sank behind the hill, everything good in the little girl's world.

# Chapter Three

"Will you stop trying to help me?" Adam snarled at Carter, who'd put a strong hand under Adam's elbow. Grant held the crutches, both brothers ready to get Adam inside so they could eat.

They didn't let go until Adam was on his feet, Grant tucking the crutches under Adam's arms. Then Carter, who'd had not just a troubled, but totally messed-up youth, looked at Adam and said, "Fuck you."

Adam made an exasperated noise. "Sorry. I'm just …"

"I know," Carter said.

Carter had dark hair, eyes that varied from hazel to light green, a tall, raw-boned body, and a mouth that could move from easygoing to a tough, mean line in a heartbeat. "But screw you if we don't want you falling on your ass," Carter went on. "Mom would get mad at *us*, and I'm not taking that for you."

"I *said* I was sorry." Adam and Carter had been scrapping since Carter had come to live with them at age thirteen. "Get over it already."

Grant fixed them both with an exasperated stare. Grant had the same coloring as Adam—brown hair, blue eyes, same solid build. The two of them looked more like twins than brothers one year apart. Grant had been wilder than Adam ever was, but in a good-natured way. While Adam had worried everyone, Grant had charmed his way out of trouble.

"Man, you got full of yourself being a Hollywood star," Grant said. "Think you're too good for us now?"

Adam wasn't in the mood for banter. "Just get me inside."

He wouldn't have minded so much stumbling around with only the family. But Bailey was coming up from the barn with Faith, and the last person he wanted seeing him like this was Bailey Farrell.

Not because he was ashamed that half his face had been through a meat grinder, but because she'd been the one who'd set him on his feet and sent him off all those years ago. Adam would never have had the success he did without Bailey, and he knew it. Now Adam was hobbling home, his mistakes maybe having killed a good man. His mentor had told him to take some time to heal, then come on back—there would always be a place for Adam.

Adam was one of the best in the business. He'd had bad crashes before, had been hurt before—worse than this, though he hadn't actually died—and had recovered and gone right back to work.

This time, thinking about going back to work clenched something in his gut. Getting into a car to

go to LAX, and then again for the drive home from
the airport in Austin, had been one of the hardest
things he'd ever done.

Now he wanted to sit on this porch, crumble to
dust, and blow away on the warm Texas wind.

It wasn't only the thought of stunt driving again
that made him sweat; it was anything that required
taking a risk. Even thinking about climbing up on his
beloved horses while he was home made him sick to
his stomach.

What the fuck was wrong with him?

Watching Bailey walk up here didn't help his
frayed nerves. "What the hell did you invite her to
dinner for?" he snapped.

"Mom did," Grant answered without heat.
"You're old friends, and Bailey's been worried about
you. Be nice to her. You had sex with her back in the
day, and she deserves a lot of niceness for that. Hell,
you should buy her an island for getting into bed
with you."

"Go screw yourself," Adam rumbled, but Grant's
teasing made him feel a little better. He'd missed
this.

He hobbled determinedly into the house. Maybe
if he got himself sitting at the table before Bailey
came in, it wouldn't be so bad. She wouldn't watch
him lurching and shaking like a little girl. Faith had
more strength than he did right now.

His mother, God bless her, knew what to do. She
always did. Olivia ignored Adam's struggles, letting
him make it across the living room to the dining
room alone, but poised to help the minute he truly
needed it. Or at least make his brothers help. Olivia,
half the height of her sons, was good at keeping the

Campbell boys in line — the only one who'd ever been able to.

It was good to see the familiar long table set with plates and silverware, napkins at the sides of the plates plus a pile in the middle — five boys weren't going to eat and not make a mess.

When Adam had been little, the plates had been mismatched, Mom putting together whatever she could. Now, thanks to the successes of her sons and the Circle C Ranch the whole family owned, the plates were a set from her favorite home decor store, the silverware new. Olivia had turned the family around since their dad's death had left them alone and dirt poor. As they'd gotten older the brothers had pitched in and helped every step of the way. They'd made it together.

Even Adam leaving for California hadn't meant he was deserting them. He'd made that clear. He came back for holidays and down time between movies — not that there was much of that. He sent a large portion of his checks home to keep the ranch going, and he was part owner in their business.

Yep, he always had a place here. Nice to have that at your back in a world where money ruled and people were hired and fired on a whim, and men like Dawson died so tightwad bean counters could save money.

Adam dropped into his chair at the far end of the table, arranging his leg the best he could. This was a smaller splint than what he'd had in the first weeks, but it was still effing awkward.

He let out his breath when he finally settled. He was here, looking down the table from the chair he'd sat in for so many years. When they'd had their first family meal after their father died, Olivia had turned to Adam and said, "You sit at the head of the table — it's your place now."

Adam, ten at the time, had been thrilled, sad, and a little scared. Being the man in the family was a lot of responsibility.

The entire family entered the dining room in a pack, surrounding Bailey and Faith, the room suddenly filled with people. When everything quieted down, Bailey ended up sitting directly on Adam's right, in the place Grant usually sat.

Somehow, Grant had moved one seat over to accommodate the extra. He didn't look one bit guilty either, the shithead. Bailey gave Adam a little smile, not at all awkward.

Damn, but she'd grown even more gorgeous than ever. She'd been nice-looking back in high school, though she'd hidden it well. Adam had discovered what other guys hadn't — that underneath the geeky bangs and glasses were fine brown eyes in a fresh face, and that her sloppy sweatshirts hid a body of sweet curves.

Bailey had grown up a lot since then. She wore her dark hair shorter now, waving back to reveal her whole face. The color on her cheeks was natural, tanned from working under the Texas sun, flushed with life.

Her eyes were brown — deep fall-into-them brown. She didn't wear glasses anymore, which meant she'd probably gone with contacts or maybe had vision surgery. Whatever she'd done, she'd learned how to throw back her shoulders and confront the world instead of ducking her head and peeking at it sideways.

Not only that, she'd become unself-consciously sexy, filling out a clinging black shirt that showed some hot cleavage. Jeans hugged her hips and one great ass.

She'd been like a budding rose ten years ago, beautiful in her own way but with potential beauty closed from the world.

Now Bailey had blossomed, and she was breathtaking.

Grant, playing nice brother today, had made sure Bailey was on Adam's right—the scars were worst on the left side of his face. Bailey looked him over with frank interest, no shirking, no embarrassment.

The last night they'd spent together, before they parted ways, she'd been under him in the dark, her smile languid as she stroked his then-long hair. They'd been young and inexperienced at sex—Adam knew that now, in spite of his supreme cockiness at the time—but it had been mind-blowing all the same. A man never forgot his first love.

When Adam caught her eye, Bailey let her smile come—that sexy, lopsided smile that said there was more to her than met the eye.

Adam's body, though pumped with pain-killers and tired as hell, responded. Bailey had been a hot little firecracker when she'd been his shy math tutor—how much more would she have to give now?

And here was Adam, bandaged and splinted, exhausted and aching, broken in body and spirit. Even so, he made the good half of his face tip up in an answering grin.

Bailey flushed, and she leaned absently forward, her breasts grazing the edge of the table. Adam couldn't help himself—he was a red-blooded Texas boy. He looked straight down her shirt.

Oh, yeah. Worth the wait.

A loud snicker erupted on his left side. Tyler, two years younger than Grant, had his elbow on the table, hand pressed to his face, laughing at his busted up but horny older brother. The others were pretending not to notice, but smirks were visible all around.

The food got set down, and Olivia and Ross, the youngest brother who was a terrific cook, took their seats. Nice that Ross was home—he was a deputy sheriff, one of the few in small River County, and worked all hours.

"Adam," Olivia said, "Say grace for us."

All eyes turned to him.

Adam dragged his gaze from Bailey's glorious bosom, cleared his throat, and stretched out his hands.

Bailey took one. Her fingers were strong, her grip firm, when years ago she'd been hesitant. Now she held his hand without shrinking, met his eye, gave him a smile, and dared him to be embarrassed about staring at her chest.

Adam flushed, grabbed Tyler's hand, and waited while the others joined up.

The lifeline that ringed the table flowed its warmth into him and lifted his heart. He was home.

He couldn't remember any prayers but one. In his movie life, they grabbed what food they could when they could. Sit-down dinners happened in restaurants surrounded by a ton of other people, and usually arranged to talk business. No time for saying grace.

Adam cleared his throat again. "Dear Lord, bless this house, this family, and this food we are about to receive. Amen."

A resounding *Amen* went around the table, then five pairs of masculine hands shot out, including his, the Campbell boys and Carter always hungry. They were polite, though, passing the dishes first to Bailey and Olivia, making sure they got their share, while Carter helped Faith fill her plate.

The room soon rang with loud voices, clattering silverware, praises to the cooks for the food, followed by the usual modest answers — *It was just a little something. We had Bailey thaw out some steaks this morning, then we threw them on the grill and scrubbed some veg. That's all.*

Olivia sat at her place at the foot of the table, her hair a sandy shade of blond that Adam knew came from the salon, but it looked good on her. She was tanned like the rest of them, her face bearing more lines now than when he'd left home, but her eyes were as lively as ever. Their mother was a strong rider, and though she didn't stunt ride, she helped with the training, kept the stables running smoothly and the horses healthy, and dealt with a lot of the business details, along with Carter, who'd proved good at it.

Now she talked with her sons and Bailey, shooting fond-mother glances down at Adam when she thought he wasn't looking. She knew Adam didn't like being coddled.

The meal was hot, juicy, tasty, savory, satisfactory. Adam didn't have much of an appetite these days, between pain and the meds, but he tried to do the food justice. Bailey joined in the dinner conversation with ease, but then, she'd been working here for almost a year, Grant had told him. She was a part of the Campbell machine now.

Adam liked that, and felt at the same time as though he were looking in through a window, watching people he didn't know. He'd been away too long.

For instance, Adam asked both Bailey and Grant, in all innocence, "So, how's Christina doing?"

Christina was two years older than Bailey, and she and Grant had been living together for a while. The two of them were well matched in looks, laughter, and a love for a good time. Christina bartended at the local bar, owned by the Farrell girls' uncle. She was part of the fabric of life in Riverbend, and so naturally, Adam asked about her.

A current of tension ran around the table. No one looked at one another; Bailey stared at her plate. The one who stiffened the most was Grant, and Adam watched him with narrowed eyes. *What the fuck?*

Faith was the one who answered. "Christina and Grant broke up," she said, as though wondering why everyone else didn't just say so. "About a year ago."

Adam bent a severe look on Grant. "A *year*? When the hell were you going to tell me?"

Grant stabbed his fork into a hunk of mashed potatoes. "You were busy. Then you were busy being dead. I didn't have the chance, and I didn't want to talk about it." Another stab. "Still don't."

Adam watched him a while longer, then gave up. Bailey glanced at Adam and sent him a quick smile. "Christina's fine. I'll tell her you asked."

Everyone breathed out and went back to eating. Tyler said quickly, to fill the silence, "We'll get you back up on Buster tomorrow, Bailey. He's the best for this."

They were obviously continuing a conversation they'd had before. "Why should she want to ride Buster?" Adam broke in. "Bobby's gentler, or Dodie. I saw you working with her today, Bailey." He forced down another bite and swallowed. The food was great, and he wished he could better appreciate it. "What are they making you do? Grooming and saddling? Warming up the horses? Because they're too lazy-ass to do it themselves?"

Bailey's smile had fire in it. "I want Buster because he'll run in a straight line while I do a vaulting leap."

Adam's fork clattered to his plate as a sudden spike of agony shot up his leg past his painkillers. "What the hell are *you* doing a vaulting leap for?"

That's what they called the trick of jumping from a running horse onto a moving object—another horse, a stagecoach, a train. It was dangerous—the timing had to be perfect, and the horse under you had to be one you could trust completely.

"They're teaching me stunt riding," Bailey answered. "More women are doing action-adventure movies these days—which I'm sure you know. They need stunt doubles that look more real than a guy in a wig." As Adam kept staring at her, she laughed. "What did you think I was doing? Mucking out stalls? Cleaning bridles? Holding horses while the menfolk get on with the business of riding?"

Yes, Adam had assumed something like that, when Grant had said, *Yeah, Bailey works here now.* It never occurred to him that Bailey would be doing the crazy-ass things he and his brothers had spent a lifetime mastering.

He should let it go. It was Bailey's life. Adam had nothing to do with it.

But again he saw the face of Dawson Sheppard, a guy who'd become his closest friend, as the pickup Dawson had been driving spun out of control, snapping into Adam on a motorcycle and sending them both through the wall.

The stunt should have been cut and dried. They'd mapped it out, walked it out, rehearsed it. Adam didn't have a clear memory of the entire thing, but the accident should not have happened. The stunt coordinator had wanted the take done before the end of the day, had rushed them into it when Adam had wanted to wait and check out a few more details. He'd been talked into starting his run, and he never should have done it. Something in Dawson's truck had gone wrong, and he'd hit Adam and then the wall at the wrong point, smashing into solid brick and sparking off explosives before they could be contained.

Adam remembered Dawson's face, his eyes staring, face bloody as the fire burned around him. His best friend, dead. Just like that. For a stupid stunt in a dumb-ass movie that would never see the light of day.

"Like hell they're teaching you stunt riding," Adam growled. "It's an easy way to die or be crippled for life. Forget it."

Bailey leaned toward him, her bosom again resting on the table. "Excuse you — I've been doing this for months already. We're careful. I know you got hurt, but..."

"But what? You think *you* won't?" The others were silent, uncomfortable. "*I'm* careful, Bailey. I'm the most careful man I know, and look what happened to me!"

"Well, I'm a woman," Bailey said, like that was a good argument or something.

"You think that makes you immune?" Adam jerked his gaze from Bailey and her sweet breasts and swept it over his stubborn-faced brothers, letting his glare land on Grant. "Look at me," he snapped. "Look at my face."

He turned his head so Grant could see the entire wreck of his left side, the scars from the grafts that went down his neck and spread under his sweatshirt.

"Is *this* what you want her to look like?" Adam's broken voice filled the room. They were all staring at him now, even Faith. They watched him in concern, except Bailey, who was flushed and angry.

Adam pointed at Bailey. "You want to take this gorgeous woman and make her look like me? What the *fuck* is wrong with you?"

He pushed himself out of his chair, lost his balance, and caught himself on the table. His crutches were against the wall, four steps away—damn it.

Bailey and Grant were out of their chairs, both reaching for the crutches, Grant backing off after a second to let Bailey bring them to him.

Adam snatched them and jerked away when Bailey tried to ease them under his arms. "Don't help me," he snarled at her. "Do *not* help me."

He saw his mother rise from her chair, either ready to yell at him or yell at the others, he wasn't sure. Adam knew he was acting like an asshole, but he didn't have time to be ashamed of his temper.

Bailey flushed again, her eyes starry with anger. Adam pushed around her—he was still strong enough to do that—and made his way to the dining-room door. To his mother he said, "Sorry. I'm not hungry. It's the meds."

They let him go, even Carter, who looked as though he wanted to tackle Adam and start beating on him. Carter wasn't one to pity a guy, which right now was easier to take than the troubled guilt from everyone else.

Adam was fine all the way to the door, which was closed. He hadn't yet mastered juggling crutches and turning doorknobs, and his idea of storming off came to an end.

A small body pushed past him, one tiny hand turning the knob for him, the other holding on to his arm. "Are you all right, Uncle Adam?"

Adam looked down at Faith, who had Carter's eyes and the soft face of the woman who'd deserted both Carter and daughter. Faith had nothing in her expression but anxiousness for Adam. Motherless Faith, being raised by her grandmother and five take-no-shit men, was the gentlest of souls.

"Sure, baby," Adam said. "I'll be fine. Don't you worry."

Faith didn't believe him. She kept her hand on his arm all the way down the hall and wouldn't turn him loose until he was in his old bedroom, lying on his bed. Faith took Adam's boot off his unsplinted leg, covered him with a blanket, kissed him on the forehead, and left him alone.

Damn the girl. Now he wanted to cry.

# Chapter Four

Buster was a good runner. No matter how much he tried to stomp on Bailey's feet or lean his weight on her when she saddled him up, he was a solid partner once they were riding out.

That is, after she stopped and retightened the cinch. Buster knew the trick of taking a deep breath when the cinch was buckled the first time, so that once he walked around and breathed out, the saddle would slide around, loose.

Grant, Tyler, and Carter always tacked up their own horses, and Bailey had fallen in with their routine. That way there was no doubt that the equipment was on exactly the way they needed it to be.

The Campbell boys and Carter had started stunt riding when they were kids—they'd been fearless, figuring out how to stand on the horses, how to vault on and jump off, how to make the horses do tricks.

Their acts had become popular in town, and then on the rodeo circuit. One day a man who'd needed horses in a movie he was shooting nearby had seen their riding, and asked Adam and his brothers, then teenagers, to help him.

They'd gained a rep for it, and got more film jobs. Adam had been the best at it, spending all his waking hours with the horses — one reason he'd started flunking school and needed Bailey's tutoring.

A man who'd worked with Adam on small-budget films had introduced him to a guy from Hollywood — Mark — who'd asked Adam to come out and assist him on some bigger movies. Adam had gone ... And that had been that.

Adam had become known for his effortless riding, and had moved from stunt riding to doing falls from buildings, and other things expensive movie stars couldn't or wouldn't do. Then he'd started stunt driving, and had been fantastic at that too.

Bailey had watched all the movies he'd done, riveted to the screen, knowing that the driver of the car that was flipping over was in fact Adam, not the movie star of the day. She'd worried sick for him, but she kept in touch with Olivia and knew that Adam had made it out of every scary stunt ... except for the last one.

She hadn't thought about stunt riding herself — she'd truly planned to just help out with the horses until she got her life back together. Bailey had learned how to cue the horses to do their tricks — rearing, bucking, falling without hurting themselves.

Most of the horses absolutely loved the job. If they didn't, they were taken out of training. No horse was pushed to do things that terrified it. The Campbells weren't cruel, and they knew that a horse without the heart for performing could let a rider down at the wrong moment, hurting itself and the rider, potentially fatally.

One day, about a month after Bailey had started work, Grant had put her on Buster to teach her how the horses were trained to buck.

Buster bucked all right, dead on cue, and Bailey had hung on fiercely, riding him until he'd finally unseated her. She'd landed on her ass in the soft dirt of the arena, as Buster had galloped away, stirrups and reins flying.

Grant had run to help her, but Bailey had sprung up, laughing and excited, and asked if she could do it again.

Grant had sat her down and told her about the dangers, and that if she wanted to do trick riding, she had to be calm, not giddy. It had taken a while for Bailey to come down from her high, but for the first time after years of anxiety, anguish, and outright unhappiness, Bailey had felt reawakened and renewed.

She understood why Adam was not happy with her, especially now that he was busted up, grieving, and in a lot of pain. But she sure as hell was not going to let him take this away from her.

Under her, Buster sped across the long stretch of ground beyond the arena where they'd been practicing. He ran straight and sure and at a steady speed. He knew his job.

Grant rode up behind her on a horse called Bobby. Buster paid no attention. He liked to run, and he knew the other horses wouldn't give him problems. They didn't dare.

Grant was pulling alongside now. The move they were practicing was for Bailey to vault from her horse to his, knock Grant from the saddle, and ride off with his horse.

Bailey watched Grant until he was beside her, stride for stride, then he pulled a little way ahead. He gave her the signal—a slight jerk of his fist—to tell her he was ready.

She leapt. Grant was in perfect position. Bailey used Buster's momentum to push herself off and get her legs over the back of Grant's horse.

She knew she'd leapt too hard even as she did it. Bailey slid over Bobby's sleek rump and kept going, heading for the ground and Bobby's pounding hooves.

As soon as she felt her balance desert her, Bailey went with the motion, letting herself fall, as Grant and Tyler had taught her. She hit the ground, but she was ready, tucking her limbs in and rolling, protecting her head.

She came to a dusty stop a few yards away, her hat gone, Texas grasses tickling her nose.

Bailey lifted her head, brushing dirt and dried grass from her face. *Damn.* She'd been trying to get this move right, and she'd been *so* close.

Buster was running happily off to the horizon, while Bobby and Grant circled back. Grant's boots landed next to Bailey as Bobby's front legs, his white socks dusty, stopped in front of her. Grant bent down, hand on Bailey's shoulder.

"You all right?"

"Fine." Bailey climbed to her feet, using Grant's arm as a lever to pull herself up. She brushed off her jeans, feeling chagrined. "I screwed that up. Sorry."

"You missed; you fell. It happens. Try again?"

Bailey ran her hands up and down her arms, shook herself out, and waited to see if she felt any pain. None came, except for what would be bruises later.

"Yep," she said.

"You ride back," Grant said, tossing her Bobby's reins. "I'll go after his royal highness."

With a nod, Bailey took the reins, accepting Grant's boost into the saddle. Grant turned around and started across the grasses as fast as his cowboy boots would let him. "Buster!" he shouted. "Get your ass back here!"

Bailey turned Bobby and rode to the arena. Buster would run, but he'd come back. He always did—when he felt like it.

Bailey let Bobby take a steady but slow pace, rewarding him for the good gallop he'd done. In the large ring ahead of her, Tyler worked another horse on the longe line. Carter came out of the house up the hill; Faith had missed the bus this morning, so Carter was driving her to school.

Carter lived here, having moved back when Faith's mother had showed up on his doorstep eight years ago, shoved Faith into his arms, and disappeared. He'd looked for Faith's mom, but never found her, and after a time, he'd been happy to give up. Finding the woman might mean having to give up Faith to her, and Carter, after his initial shock, had fallen in love with his daughter and become fiercely protective of her.

The other brothers had moved out and back in several times, depending on their circumstances. Currently, Ross lived in a small house in town, near the sheriff's department. Grant, who'd been living here since his breakup with Christina, had recently bought a trailer a few miles down the road. Tyler had been living with a girlfriend until they'd broken up a month ago, and he'd moved back home. Tyler, who loved the ladies, was in danger of going through every woman in the county—he'd have to start repeating soon or move to a city. Of course he'd lost a girl he loved to tragedy when he was very young, probably the reason he'd never settled down.

The Campbell's ranch house was big, added on to once the training business had started making money, improved again when Adam had begun pulling in bigger fees for his movie work.

As kids, the boys had shared several big bedrooms—these days each brother had his own little hideaway in the house, with a suite for Carter and Faith.

Now Adam had moved back in. For how long?

Adam was standing outside the ring, watching Tyler, as Bailey rode up. Tyler saw her coming, but he moved his attention back to the horse he was working, a filly he'd acquired a few weeks ago.

Bailey slowed Bobby to a walk, letting him saunter along as she studied Adam.

Adam might have crutches under his arms, and his face might be a healing wreck, but he stood straight and tall. His leg in its brace—bright blue plastic—was bent at the knee, but his head was up, his shoulders and back holding power. He didn't try to hide his scars, though he'd put on a wide-brimmed black cowboy hat to shield himself from the late August sun.

Adam turned his head to look at her, and the air burned between them.

Bailey could have walked on with Bobby, taking him into the covered arena beyond to cool him down and wait for Grant. But she for some reason pulled to a halt next to Adam and slid from the saddle.

The fall had stiffened her, and her leg bent as she landed. She stumbled, biting back a swear word.

A firm hand caught her beneath the arm and kept her on her feet. Warmth shot through Bailey as Adam held her with a strength his injuries hadn't been able to take away. He bent his head to look into her face, the brim of his hat darkening his eyes to cobalt.

He said nothing, only gazed at her, while Bailey tried to steady herself, his grip not letting her fall.

Bobby nuzzled Adam's shoulder. Adam couldn't hold on to the crutches and Bailey and move from the horse at the same time, so he released Bailey to give Bobby's nose a stroke.

"I saw you fall," Adam said, his look stern. "What happened?" His voice was gravelly, commanding.

Bailey tried to shrug, but her shoulder hurt. "I miscalculated. I missed the horse but hit the ground."

Adam's brows slammed together. She expected him to shout at her as he had last night, to tell her how stupidly dangerous stunt riding was. Instead, Adam lifted his hand and brushed it across Bailey's cheek.

# Chapter Five

Adam's touch was hotter than sunshine. His gaze was on her face, where Bailey's skin stung — she must have scraped herself in the fall.

Adam's fingers moved, brushing, incredibly gentle. When he'd steadied her, his grip had been hard; now his touch was feather light.

Bailey should pull away, say she was all right, walk Bobby to the covered arena or back to find Grant. But she couldn't move.

Adam continued to brush her cheek, his fingers tracing the contours of her face. Just as Bailey began to lean into his touch, he moved his hand to her shoulder and then down her long sleeve. Bailey always made sure her arms were covered when she rode with the brothers, knowing most of the time she'd end up on the ground. Adam's hand was warm through the fabric, as though the barrier between his skin and hers didn't exist.

The horse in the ring thundered past, cantering at the end of the line Tyler held. Adam jerked, and his gaze flicked to Bailey's. They shared a long look, Bailey flushing, Adam's eyes unmoving.

His hand fell away, back to the crutch. "Dirt," he said, by way of explanation.

"Yeah." Bailey rubbed more dust from her sleeve.

"You want to be a stunt rider, you'll be covered with it," Adam said, voice hard. "And bruises. And blood."

Bailey finished brushing herself off and put one fist on her hip. "If you're going to tell me it's no job for a woman, I'll yell at you. There are plenty of stuntwomen out there."

"I know," Adam said. "I've dated a few. We compared injuries."

Bailey had a sudden flash of Adam, naked on a bed, another woman drawing her fingers over his flesh as he told her what part of himself he'd hurt and how he'd done it. The woman would purr as she showed him her scars in return.

Something burned in Bailey's gut. "There you go, then," was all she could think of to say.

"Doesn't mean you should do it," Adam said. "The women I knew didn't last very long. They got hurt too bad and had to retire, or they got sick of the dumb-ass dangerous things directors wanted them to do. That's the life, Bailey."

"I never said I was running out to Hollywood to dive off buildings," Bailey returned. "I heard *you* took a twenty-story fall and barely made your landing bag. Your mom was kind of green in the face for a whole week after that."

Adam flushed, which made his scars stand out. "Someone repositioned the airbag when I was climbing to my mark. That's another thing that happens—you prepare all you can, and then some asshole nearly kills you. That's also the life."

"Didn't see you running home, though, to reassure her."

Adam took a step closer, his crutch brushing Bailey's leg. Bobby, still held by Bailey, watched with equine interest. "I'm here now. I made it. You might not."

"So, you're saying it's all right for you to nearly be killed and make your whole family worried sick, but I can't learn a few simple stunts, because it upsets *you*?"

His look turned to a glare. "'Scuse me? Where are you getting that from? It's fucking dangerous—doesn't matter who's doing it."

"I got that from your diatribe at the dinner table last night. Yelling at your brothers for trying to hurt me." Bailey lifted her finger, pointing it at his face. "It's *my* choice, Adam. Not your brothers'. Not yours. We all decided it was your meds talking, and to leave you alone. But what you said wasn't fair."

Adam's flush deepened, but he decided to grow angry instead of apologize.

But then, the great Adam Campbell had never apologized. People did things for him because he was good-looking, charming, and had those gorgeous blue eyes. That's why Bailey had run to him the last month in high school, saying she'd help him graduate—asking nothing in return.

"My meds are to keep me alive and fix me," Adam growled. "My point was that you'll end up like me, and that's a stupid place to be."

Bailey knew exactly what he meant—he'd been deeply hurt, had lost a friend, and didn't want to watch others go through that. She was the one who should apologize, tell him she understood, be nice to him.

That was tough, though. She'd been the nice girl all the way up until she'd come home a day early from a conference and found the woman she thought was her closest friend snuggled in bed with her husband.

"Or you could trust your brothers to take care of me," Bailey said. "You could trust *me*."

Adam took another step toward her. He was close enough for the brim of his hat to shade her face. "Sweetheart, what I learned in the last ten years was that I trust myself and no one else. I'd have been dead a while ago, if I hadn't."

*Nice* was heading off to the horizon to catch up with Buster. "I see. We should all do what you say, because you've proved yourself?"

"Damn straight."

Adam was a head taller than Bailey, and when he stood this close, his warmth was all over her. His eyes were like chips of the sky, but glittering now, full of rage with a darkness behind it.

Bailey drew a breath, flustered but determined not to show it. "You know, don't you, that if it hadn't been for me, you'd have had to spend another year in school and missed your golden opportunity to go out and throw yourself off horses, buildings, moving cars ..."

Adam's anger flickered as incredulity took its place. "What, now I owe all my success to *you*?"

"Damn straight."

Adam stared at her a while longer, then something like amusement entered his eyes. "Well, you grew a pair, didn't you, sweetheart? Threw away your geeky glasses and got some stones."

"Seriously?" Bailey looked straight at him, no wavering. "*Stones*? And stop calling me *sweetheart*. I'm not one of your Hollywood floozies."

"Floozies." Adam's amusement grew. "Is that what you kids call them these days? I called them *actresses* — actually I called them by their names."

Bailey clenched her hands. The last thing she wanted to talk about were the women Adam had gone out with. He'd gotten photographed with a beautiful starlet — or two — on his arm quite often. Gossip magazines showed pictures of him escorting these ladies to clubs, parties, award ceremonies, and wherever. Adam always looked good in the photos. In a tux, with his cowboy hat, he was devastating.

"I'm sure you did," Bailey said, unable to think of anything wittier. "Anyway, I have nothing to do with your life out there — or your life here. Anymore. Whatever."

Adam's humor vanished, the dark anger rising again. "Good. You don't need to be in that life, or with me, one of the walking dead."

Bailey knew she should turn around and storm off. That's obviously what he wanted her to do. Or admit she didn't know what she was talking about, that Adam was right about everything, and duck her head, turn away, and go.

She stood her ground. She continued to look Adam right in the eyes, though it was increasingly difficult to do it. Adam wasn't a pushover, never had been. Years of putting himself in danger had made him more unyielding than before.

They might have stood there for the rest of the day, while the sun beat down on them and dust from the ring coated them, if Grant hadn't come riding up on Buster, the recalcitrant horse found.

"Ready to go again, Bailey?" Grant asked.

Tyler had walked to the edge of the ring, sun glinting on hair that was a lighter shade of brown than his brothers'. "She will be as soon as Adam stops being a shithead."

"Adam's fine," Bailey snapped, suddenly irritated with them. They needed to cut Adam some slack. "But, yeah, I'm ready. I'll get it this time."

Adam didn't say a word. He simply held her with his gaze while Grant dismounted, until she turned around, took Buster's reins, and mounted him, this time refusing Grant's leg-up.

Adam was still watching her, nothing weak about him, as she turned Buster, nudged him forward, and guided him once more out to the open fields.

\*\*

*Five weeks later …*

Five weeks of healing plus grueling physical therapy and painkillers and doctor's visits—Adam essentially had to live three days a week in Austin to go to the specialist his mentor, Mark, had set up for him.

Carter, surprisingly, was the one who ended up ferrying Adam back and forth. While Carter got along the best with Ross, there had always been a little friction between Carter and the two oldest Campbell brothers. Grant and Adam were close, best friends, didn't matter how far apart they lived from each other, but Carter had been hard to get to know.

Adam admitted he hadn't let Carter into the twosome when he'd first arrived. But then, Carter had been unhappy, resentful, and difficult, only gentling himself for Ross, who'd been ten when Carter had come to live with them. Carter had protected Ross, walking him to school, keeping him safe from bullies, not minding his incessant questions and little-kid prattle.

Adam had left home before he and Carter had grown into adults—Carter had been a snarling sixteen-year-old the autumn Adam had moved to California.

Carter had calmed down a lot, Adam had seen during his visits home, especially since Faith had come along, but Adam had never really connected with him fully. Even now, during the two-hour drives from Riverbend to Austin, he and Carter didn't talk about much, mainly sticking to topics like the horses, Faith, and who'd moved into or out of town while Adam had been in Los Angeles.

Regardless, Adam liked the chance he had now to hang out with Carter as a brother, the two of them no longer antagonists. Not that Carter was all touchy-feely. He spoke his mind, and whenever he thought Adam was being a dickhead, he said so.

When Adam finally was released from physical therapy and had his meds cut down to acetaminophen when he needed it, he celebrated by going out to Riverbend's one bar. It was officially named *Sam's Tavern*, but the entire town simply called it *The Bar*.

Carter drove him again. Olivia stayed home with Faith and told the boys to go have fun. Adam looked forward to drinking an actual beer, spending time with his brothers, and catching up with old friends.

Old friends who weren't Bailey. Adam had gone through the five healing weeks avoiding her as much as possible. Easy enough, with him in Austin so much. At one point, Bailey had taken off to New Mexico with Grant and Tyler to do a movie shoot for one of the small studios the brothers did contract work for. Adam worried like crazy the whole time — even though Grant had assured him that Bailey wasn't doing any dangerous stunts, only helping with the horses and doing background riding.

Still, Adam was much relieved when she returned, happy and sunburned, tired but excited by the experience. He'd watched her from afar as she'd helped the brothers unload the horses, before he'd taken off for Austin again.

Carter, as usual, said little tonight as he drove the five miles from the ranch into town and through it to reach the bar. The sun was going down, touching their faces and the old scars on Carter's arms from where drug dealers used to torture him. Carter had never revealed all that had happened to him, but Olivia had not let up until Carter had explained the scars. The dealers he'd worked for had tested the sharpness of their knives on him, as well as cutting patterns into his skin that meant he belonged to them. The scars had faded somewhat, and Carter hadn't talked about them since.

It was Saturday night, the bar full. Everyone in town came here if they didn't head out for the cities or to the lakes over the weekend.

Adam walked with Carter from Carter's pickup through the maze of vehicles toward the thump of music. Darkness now coated the sky, the lights of the lot and the bar bright against the night.

Adam had long since abandoned the crutches, but he still walked with a slight limp. That would go away with more work, his physical therapist told him, but he had to put up with it for now.

Adam's face was another matter. He couldn't hide the mottled scarring the fire and then the grafts had left unless he wore a bag over his head.

As he walked into the bar through the crowd, he saw people look at him and away, embarrassed to be caught staring at his ruined face.

Well, they'd have to get used to it. This was what Adam looked like now. He hated it, but what the hell was he supposed to do? Hide in his room the rest of his life?

Christina Farrell, dispensing drinks behind the bar, looked up when Adam and Carter came in. She sent them a huge, warm grin, grabbed the rope of the ship's bell that had hung there for decades, and clanged the bell enthusiastically.

"It's Adam!" she yelled as everyone in the bar turned toward the clamor. "Let's hear it for Adam Campbell!"

A cheer went up, along with whoops and yells, as beers and drinks were lifted his way. Adam started to relax. They weren't condemning him, or reveling in his misfortune. His old friends were welcoming him home.

Adam waved in thanks as he pushed his way to the bar and slapped both hands to the top of it. "Gimme a beer," he said to Christina. "I've got a lot of catching up to do, so keep 'em coming."

Christina renewed her smile as she pulled the tap to fill a glass. She had the same curly dark hair as Bailey, though she wore it short, and she didn't hide her ample curves behind long-sleeved button-down shirts and jeans. Her tight white tank top and cutoff shorts hugged everything she had.

"You've had a rough time, Bailey says." Christina slid Adam the full glass, the head not too tall, not too skimpy. "You doing okay?"

"Better," Adam said. A hell of a lot better. He no longer felt as though he'd fall over dead the moment he stood up. Bodily, he was healing. In his mind, not so much.

"Everyone thinks you're awesome," Christina said, wiping condensation from the wooden bar top. "We all thought about getting you a card, but figured you wouldn't like that."

"My friends know me well," Adam said.

And yet, so many faces from his childhood were gone. This was ranching and farming country, and if the land couldn't pay, farms were sold or just went bust, and people moved to the cities or to the oil towns out west of here, looking for work. Austin and Midland grew while Riverbend shrank.

Adam put the regret of that aside as he lifted his beer and set it to his lips. Tickle of foam, stream of liquid into his mouth, the savory taste of wheat, the bite of hops. Damn, how he'd missed it. He closed his eyes, swallowing, and took another long, luxurious sip.

Christina laughed at him. "You going to drink it or buy it lingerie?"

Adam gave her a faint smile and set down the mug. "It's been a hell of a recovery. Hell of a crash."

"I heard. I'm sorry."

Adam shrugged. He closed his eyes for another sip when laughter floated to him—feminine, sexy laughter that had imprinted itself onto his heart years ago.

Adam turned his head and saw Bailey. His mouth, which he'd opened to put more beer into, stayed that way.

He'd just been thinking about Bailey's concealing shirts and pants, but she wasn't wearing those tonight. Her legs were sleek and curved under a thigh-hugging skirt; her arms were bared by a tight little shirt with cap sleeves. The dim light glistened on her dark hair, which she'd pulled back into a ponytail, revealing the entire loveliness of her face.

She was at one of the pool tables, cue in her hand, laughing up at a man with black hair and green eyes. As Adam watched, his blood growing hotter by the second, the black-haired man slid his arm around Bailey's waist, leaned down, and kissed her on the lips.

Adam was off the barstool before he realized his feet had hit the floor. He grabbed Carter as Carter turned from friends to join Adam.

Carter gave Adam a narrow-eyed stare, glancing down at Adam's fingers locked around his biceps, but Adam didn't let go.

"Tell me," Adam said, his jaw so tight he feared it would break, "what the *fuck* is Bailey doing here with *Kyle Malory*?"

# Chapter Six

Carter jerked himself from Adam's grasp. Adam knew Carter was holding himself back from punching his older brother in the face, reining in his temper with effort. Spoke a lot about the change in Carter—in the old days, Carter would have simply punched.

"She's going out with him, because Christina is going out with Ray," Carter said, words clipped. Ray was Kyle's older brother.

Adam forgot about his beer and the simple enjoyment of it. "When the hell were you going to tell me about this?"

"It's only been a couple of weeks." Carter scowled at him. "And anytime anyone brought up Bailey, you changed the subject. Your own fault."

"*Shit.*"

As Adam watched, Bailey pulled away from the kiss before it got too hot—she had always been modest. Then she stunned Adam senseless by bending over to take a shot at the pool table, her skirt molding to the finest ass in the bar.

Adam stared at it until he realized he couldn't take his eyes off her. He made himself turn away to the bar. "Christina!"

Christina came back to him, smiling like a good hostess. "Another already? You haven't finished the first one."

Carter, who'd followed, broke in. "He's going to ask you about the Malorys," he said with a growl. "Like it's his business."

Christina lost her smile. "Come on, Adam. You know how I felt about Grant, but it just didn't work out. It was a painful decision for us, so no, I don't want to talk about it. Ray and me have been friends a long time. Kyle and Bailey too. It's nice for me — I get to spend more time with my sister."

Adam hadn't been worried about Christina and Grant, though surprised they'd broken up and sorry the relationship had ended. Grant still hadn't told him about it, being very prickly on the subject.

Adam realized that Christina had no idea that he'd only been thinking about Bailey — thinking about her as though what they'd shared all those years ago had meant something.

Again, *shit.*

"Don't be mad, Adam," Christina said. "You know I love all you guys, and I want us to stay friends."

"What?" Adam realized he was glaring at her. "No, no. It's cool. It's ... Don't worry about it."

Christina gave him a nod, looking relieved. She started to turn away, then she stopped and pinned him with a sharp stare. Adam sipped his beer, willing her to go, but she kept watching him. Finally her face softened, she smiled to herself, and turned to serve a man farther down the bar.

Carter had taken his beer and left Adam, to find his friends. He hung out with guys he'd known a long time, who were not necessarily fans of the Campbells. Olivia had never forced Carter to make certain friends and leave others alone, but let him fall into relationships that suited him. The boys he'd taken up with in school were like him—seeking to figure out where they belonged in the world. They weren't bad guys, just rough around the edges and suspicious of close families, probably because they'd never been part of one. Carter was now, but he never forgot what it was to be an outsider.

Tyler had just arrived, and was already flirting his ass off with a young woman who gave him coy looks. *Coy, my ass. She'd be in bed with Tyler before midnight.*

To hell with it. Adam took up his beer and walked over to the pool tables, trying not to limp too much.

Bailey was in the middle of taking another shot. She looked up, saw Adam, and her cue slipped. Balls rolled all over the place, but none found pockets.

"Adam." Bailey straightened up, flushing. "You look ... better."

"Thanks," Adam said dryly. "I can walk upright. How y'all doing?" The group around the table consisted of Malorys—Kyle and Ray, and one of their cousins from Lampasas—plus the cousin's date, and Bailey.

Ray gave Adam a nod, neither friendly nor unfriendly, but Kyle looked Adam up and down.

"Adam. Man, you really did a number on yourself." His look was sympathetic, but also curious for the details.

Kyle and Adam had been rivals since the first grade. They'd competed with each other to be the best rider, best athlete, best fighter, the best in everything ... except academic achievement. Their teachers claimed the two competed to be the biggest screw-ups in town, and they hadn't been wrong.

Even at six years old, Adam and Kyle had fought over women. Mindy Walters, a blond and beautiful first-grader had the two boys coming to blows the first day of school. Neither Kyle nor Adam would have known what to do with a woman if they'd caught one, but both knew they had to be the one who walked Mindy to her bike and carried her book bag. Mindy had grown up to become a famous round-the-world photojournalist, leaving Riverbend far behind. Rumor had it that she was gay, but she'd been their first conquest.

Not their last. Adam and Kyle had tried to out-macho each other over every woman since. Except Bailey. Not in high school, anyway. Only Adam had discovered the beauty behind the shyness of gorgeous Christina Farrell's little sister.

Now Bailey had blossomed, and Kyle had moved right in.

Adam gave a nod at Kyle's assessment of his injuries, but he looked Kyle right in the man's too-green eyes. Guys shouldn't have eyes like that — all the Malory men did — and women were all over them for it.

Kyle caught the challenge in Adam's gaze, and his horrified but slightly superior sympathetic look faded. He understood. Didn't matter that Adam looked chewed up and spit out. The rivalry was still on.

If Bailey had caught the exchange, she said nothing. She continued talking as though she and Adam hadn't snarled at each other the last time they'd had a conversation, five weeks ago, and hadn't spoken much since. "You're done with the physical therapy, right?" she asked. "Everyone will be glad to have you home more."

"Yeah, Carter's getting tired of driving me around," Adam said. If she wanted to be all friendly, he could play too. "I'll have to get me a truck or something, so I can drive myself." The thought of driving made cold sweat trickle down his back, but he'd have to get over it.

"Tyler and Grant will be glad to see you riding again," Bailey went on, still giving him that false little smile. Too bad any smile made her beautiful. "The Fall Festival is coming up."

The Fall Festival was a county fair with a small-scale rodeo held every year in late October. It involved exhibition riding and competitions in roping, cattle cutting, and bull riding as well pleasure riding classes for the amateurs and kids. The Campbells had been in every Fall Festival since Adam could remember. So had the Malorys.

The Campbells showed off their trick riding every year, which was how they'd been discovered. The Malory boys were champion bull riders, and this was also their chance to show off. The Fall Festival was supposed to be for friendly competition, but the Malorys and the Campbells always played to win.

Since Adam was better, the town would expect him to join his brothers in the exhibition riding. That is, if Adam didn't race back to California now that his physical therapy was done and the doctors had cleared him to work.

That was his choice—go back to the life that had killed Dawson, or stay here and be a local hero on horseback.

He wanted to throw up. Maybe he shouldn't have been too quick to grab a beer.

The idea of climbing on a horse and jumping and whirling around until he was dizzy made him as clammy as the thought of driving again. People claimed the brain erased the immediate trauma of an accident, blotting the memories, but Adam remembered too much. Spinning, fire, shouting, the horrible noise as everything fell apart ...

The next thing he knew, Bailey was next to him, shoving a pool cue into his nerveless fingers.

"I'm losing," she said, looking up into his face. "Why don't you take my place?"

She was covering for him. Adam realized he'd stopped moving, stopped breathing, and now the air rushed back into his lungs. Kyle and Ray were watching him—looking for weakness? Or wondering whether they'd have to call an ambulance?

Bailey's soft eyes said, *Trust me. Hold on to me, and I'll get you through this.*

She'd said more or less the same thing years ago, when Adam asked for her help. She'd become very defensive of him, furious with others who called him a waste of good talent, a disgrace to his mother and family, or just a plain dumb-ass. She'd gone to bat for him, and hadn't been wrong when she'd said that because of her, he'd been able to take his dream job out in glitter-land.

Adam swallowed. He gripped the cue and took another long breath. "Sure." He pulled his gaze from Bailey with difficulty and pinned it on Kyle. "Eight ball? What are the stakes?"

Kyle wanted to say *Bailey*. Adam saw it in the other man's eyes. Also *She's with me, so suck it*.

Bailey might be with Kyle now, tonight. But tonight wasn't forever.

Kyle shrugged, pretending he didn't care. "Hundred bucks?"

"Make it two hundred," Adam said. "And hold on to your ass, because I'm gonna kick it."

"Talking don't make it real, Campbell." Kyle gestured to the table. "Be my guest."

Ray started collecting balls, grinning as though enjoying himself hugely. Why not? He'd stolen Grant's girlfriend and was now watching Kyle steal Adam's. The Malory brothers were getting, as Adam's mom liked to say, too big for their britches. Time to take them down a peg.

Adam waited for Ray to set all the balls in the triangle, then he positioned it himself, removed the rack, placed the cue ball, and shot.

The cue ball smacked into the cluster with a crack like a gunshot, and balls burst across the table. Two solids fell into pockets, and Adam straightened up. "Like I said, hold on."

He moved to shoot again, highly aware of Bailey standing at the corner of the table, that skirt beckoning his gaze. She had grown up, that was for sure, all curves, nothing hidden.

Kyle went to stand next to her, his cue upright between them. As Adam worked the table, that cue and Kyle got closer and closer to Bailey. Kyle didn't give a rat's ass, Adam saw, who won. The man had Bailey, all that mattered.

The distraction made Adam play less well than he should have. One shot had his solid balls lined up against a long rail, the cue ball in an awkward position behind them. He might click one in if he hit it just right, but he'd have to lean lengthwise along the table to do it.

He lowered himself to the table, positioning his cue between fingers that were callused in places, smooth from burns in others.

He had the shot, but as he drew back, his bad leg folded under him. He'd had problems with cramping at the stupidest times, and now was one.

Adam slipped. His cue tapped the white ball, which rolled a few halfhearted inches and stopped. He ended up mostly on the table, his cue clattering to the floor, his right leg not working, his nose on the felt.

Two soft hands landed on him, and a wash of feminine scent brushed him. Not perfume — the good smell of Bailey.

"You all right?"

Her voice was his lifeline. A long time ago, when Adam had been leaning on his truck, the last vehicle in the school's parking lot, knowing he had to go home and tell his mom he was on the verge of flunking out, a younger version of the same voice had come to him. He'd had his arms folded on the truck's closed door, head bowed, Adam ashamed and unhappy and not knowing what to do about it.

*Adam?* the sweet voice had said. *You all right?*

*Yeah,* he'd said. *Yeah, I'm fine.*

Bailey had known better. *I can help you.* She'd stammered a little, nervous. *If you want. I'm good at math. I could maybe teach you …*

He'd turned around and seen an angel. Not the nerdy girl other kids made fun of, with her sloppy clothes, heavy hair, and thick glasses. She hugged her books to her chest, which was probably why Adam had never noticed what a rack she had. The brown eyes peering at him through the glasses were wide, honest, and caring.

Instead of blowing her off or growing insulted, Adam had grabbed on to the line she'd thrown him. *Sure,* he'd said, as though it were unimportant. *Doing anything right now?*

And took her home with him. They'd sat on the porch of his mom's house and opened the books. Bailey had come over every day after that, patiently teaching Adam math, and then English and history and anything else he'd struggled with.

Adam remembered the day the numbers in the math equations had stopped dancing around and settled down into something he understood. He'd jumped up, euphoria flooding him, enlightenment in his grasp. He'd wanted to shout and punch the air, but instead he'd grabbed Bailey and kissed her.

And his eyes had been opened. He'd kissed her thoroughly, there on the porch where they'd been alone, pressing her against a post, his hands on her waist, then her back, and finally, her breasts. Her first kiss, he could tell, but her enthusiasm for it was better than cool experience.

The next day, when the family went out, leaving Adam behind to study, he'd sneaked Bailey into his bedroom. He remembered uncovering her layer by layer—lush breasts, lickable legs, sexy ass, her warm smile lighting her eyes.

It hadn't been his first time—Adam had lost his virginity at fourteen with an ardent sixteen-year-old cheerleader from a rival school—but his first time with Bailey had been seared upon his brain, never to be forgotten.

He'd touched her, kissed her body, brought her to her first pleasure with his hands. Then, when she was open with the shock of her first orgasm, he'd slipped inside. Beautiful, tight Bailey had closed around him, embracing him with her arms and her body.

That had been the first encounter in their short but intense affair—every day they'd managed to find a place to be together, to make love, to lie afterward in the sunshine, and talk and laugh. Bailey could laugh about anything.

Adam was later surprised he'd found time to graduate with all the sex going on, but he'd made it, and Bailey had gotten him there. Her smile as he'd walked up to receive his diploma had bolstered him more than the piece of paper the principal had slapped into his hand.

The memories had been burned onto Adam's body, and now, at Bailey's touch, at her words of concern, he remembered every moment.

Adam's heart constricted into a tight knot and hurt like hell when it expanded again.

"I'm fine," Adam snapped, jerking himself back to reality. "My damn leg just seizes up."

A stronger grip landed on his shoulders. Bailey's touch fell away as Kyle lifted Adam to his feet. Kyle stepped back immediately, which was a good thing, because Adam felt his fist balling.

"It sucks," Kyle said. "Took me forever to get over a broken foot and ribs after a bull crushed me in the chute. Go ahead and take another shot."

"Screw that," Adam growled. "I don't need a pity do-over. You go for it. It won't help you."

Kyle gave him an I'll-make-you-eat-those-words glance, and moved to the table. Adam looked on the floor for his cue, but it was gone.

Bailey had it. She handed it to him without words, compassion and understanding in her eyes.

Something lodged in Adam's throat. He couldn't talk, couldn't apologize for snarling at her. Bailey stood beside him, regardless of his temper, as though ready to catch him if he fell again.

Kyle had better hurry and win the stupid game. Adam had to get out of here before he did something dumb-ass like grab Bailey and drag her off to have his way with her in a corner. He could barely move, and he'd only end up making a fool of himself. Kyle was right about one thing. This well and truly sucked.

Adam ended up winning the game. Kyle was down to his last ball, then he tried to bank the cue ball into the last striped ball on the table. His aim was off a hair, and the target ball bounced away from the pocket, to the groans of the crowd that had gathered.

Adam stepped up, sank the last solid balls, and slammed the black eight ball into the corner pocket.

The crowd cheered and broke up, and Kyle shrugged with an oh-well look.

"Pay up outside," Adam said. Christina would throw them out if she saw them blatantly exchanging money. Her uncle's bar wasn't a casino, she'd say.

Kyle nodded and extended his hand. "Good game."

Adam clasped it, making his grip as strong as Kyle's. Kyle increased the pressure. So did Adam. They'd shaken like this many times.

"Yeah, good game," Adam said.

They finally broke the clasp when both their hands were in danger of breaking. Kyle shot Adam a grin, in no way worried about the loss.

Of course not. Kyle got to walk away with his arm around Bailey's shoulders. She looked back at Adam and gave him a warm smile.

Kicked him right in the gut.

**

The next morning, Sunday, Bailey went to church, then ended up at Christina's house for the afternoon. Christina had worked late the night before, closing the bar, and she was just rising when Bailey arrived. Bailey had a key to Christina's place, so she let herself in—first checking whether Ray Malory's truck was parked in front.

It wasn't, so Bailey went inside to hear Christina's shower running. She poured herself an iced tea and settled down on the sofa to wait and think about Adam, warm under her arm when she'd tried to help him from the pool table. He'd been angry and lashed out, but she couldn't blame him. He was used to being strong, and weakness in himself made him furious.

She'd been distracted the rest of the night and had decided to go home early. Kyle had seen nothing amiss, and had dropped her off at home, only saying good night when she didn't ask him to stay.

The shower went off. After a few minutes, Christina wandered out in shorts and tank top, plopping onto a chair and dangling her legs over its arm.

"I always think better when my legs are shaved." Christina pointed the toes of one foot to the ceiling and ran her fingers along her calf.

Bailey grinned at her sister. "You mean they weren't shaved for Ray last night?"

Christina shook her head. "We didn't go out. He's taking me to dinner tonight. When I'm that tired after I close I don't want to do anything but sleep. By myself, I mean. I might snore. Or drool."

Bailey settled back on the sofa and sipped her tea. Since she'd moved home from Austin, she and Christina had spent their Sundays together. Their parents had moved when her father had taken a job in San Antonio a few years back, but Christina had remained in Riverbend, and Bailey had been drawn back here when she thought of *home*. They'd never talked about why, but maybe it was time.

"Seriously, Christina, what happened between you and Grant?" Bailey asked. "You two were fused. I come back here and find you broken up, and you never told me why, not in any detail. I didn't want to pry, considering what happened to me—I sure as hell got sick of people asking me if I was all right. But really—what happened?"

Christina lost her dreamy look and pain flashed through her eyes. "It's complicated."

"Not good enough. I'm your little sister. That means you're obligated to tell me everything."

Christina swung her legs down and sat up straight. Her eyes still held pain, but also fiery determination. "All right," she said. "I'll give you the whole deal. But not for free. When I'm done, you're going to tell me all about what's going on with you and Adam."

# Chapter Seven

Bailey's face went hot. "What do you mean, with me and Adam? There's nothing going on. At all."

Christina's brown eyes sparkled. "Oh, right. Sweetie, last night, when Adam saw you with Kyle, he looked like he wanted to murder everyone in the bar, starting with Kyle. He was furious. At first, I thought he was mad at me for going out with Ray, but I was totally wrong." Her smile widened. "Come on. What happened?"

"Nothing." Bailey knew her cheeks must be bright red — she'd never been able to hide a blush — and she struggled for words. "Adam doesn't want anything to do with me. He's pissed off because I'm learning to stunt ride, which is totally understandable. He got hurt, and his friend died. He *should* be pissed off. He yelled at me about it, and hasn't spoken to me since. And Kyle is ... nice." *Not demanding. Not intense. A relief.*

Christina burst out laughing. "If Kyle Malory heard himself called *nice*, he'd shit a brick. Kyle's a bad boy. So is Adam. I'm sensing a pattern here."

"Yeah, well, I married a respectable guy, didn't I?" Bailey said darkly. "He graduated at the top of his class, got an advanced degree, went to work every day, and church on Sunday. And he turned out to be a total bastard. Never trust a guy who spends more money on a tie than most people spend on food for a week. I thought he was being sweet to me, telling me to invite my girlfriend over more often, letting her hang out with us. He must have been laughing about how stupid I was. That's not something you get over very fast. I'm not ready for another relationship — with anyone."

Christina had risen during this diatribe, and now she thrust a champagne flute into Bailey's hand, filled with bubbling orange juice.

"You look like you could use a mimosa. It's Sunday. We'll call it brunch."

Bailey didn't usually enjoy sweet drinks, but this morning, she gripped the flute in tight fingers and took a long swallow. Anyway, orange juice had so much vitamin C.

Christina sat down again with a glass of iced tea. Christina didn't drink, saying she'd tended bar long enough to see what heavy drinking did to people. She wasn't afraid to cut off patrons in the bar, no matter how angry they became. She knew everyone in town, and one threat to call the angry person's mom usually calmed them down enough for their friends to get them home.

"Listen, honey," Christina said. "What your ex did was a dirty, rotten trick. I bet he didn't think you were stupid at all—he was just relieved he got away with it as long as he did. You caught him and exposed him for what he really was—a cheater and a liar. I know you feel burned and hurt, and you should. But you're not in the wrong here—you never were. You're home now, and all *our* sympathies are with you."

Bailey didn't say anything for a time, though she warmed at Christina's words. Two years had passed since the awful day she'd found Lawrence in bed with the woman she'd known since they'd been roommates in college, the woman who'd taught Bailey how to dress and do her hair and leave her mousy high-school look behind.

Bailey had walked out and found a lawyer that day—no hesitation, or she might have chickened out, forgiven Lawrence, and let herself be walked on as usual.

Legal proceedings had taken time, especially since Lawrence had tried to fight it, but eventually, Bailey had a document that said she was free of her marriage. She'd returned to Riverbend to lick her wounds, and only when she'd taken up riding with the Campbell brothers had she climbed out of the pit of gloom her life had become. Now she woke each morning looking forward to the day instead of dreading it.

Watching Adam walk back into her life—even on crutches—had woken her up even more. Her decade in Austin was becoming a passing event, an aberrant blip, while *this* life was real.

"Now," Christina went on. "I'm going to tell you that the Campbells aren't like that at all. They might be bad boys, and they might love the ladies, but they're not cheating bastards. You get what you get, nothing hidden."

Bailey took another sip of the mimosa, bubbles dancing on her tongue. "If that's true, why aren't you still with Grant?"

Christina lost her wise older sister look and slumped back in her chair. "It really was complicated, Bailey. Not just one thing. Everyone in town thinks I got mad because of all the buckle bunnies chasing him, but it wasn't that. Grant doesn't care about groupies. But it ... " She paused, closing her eyes, true pain on her face. "It's hard to put into words."

"Hey," Bailey said, her heart squeezing. "If you don't want to talk about it, don't. But like you said to me, you have all my sympathy. Grant doesn't know what he's throwing away."

"No, don't blame him." Christina opened her eyes, tears in them. "It's not his fault, not entirely. We lived together for five years. We talked about getting married—Grant wanted to. But he wants kids. A big family. So do I—I love kids. But in five years, none came along." She gave Bailey a wan smile. "Believe me, we tried. Every day. No one can say we held back in the sack. We never used any kind of birth control, and the sex was ... well, it's *Grant*. Mind-blowing, every single time. But, no matter what we did, I never got pregnant. We went to doctors who said there was nothing wrong with either of us. But we each blamed ourselves, beating ourselves up about it, and then we started blaming each other. Then we were fighting about everything we could think of. After a while we were unhappy when we were together and super-tense when we were apart. Finally, we decided we should let each other go. He said it first, but I'd been thinking it. We were stopping each other from getting on with our lives. It was a relief."

The last word was choked out, her voice clogged with tears. Christina quickly set down her iced tea and put her hand over her eyes.

Bailey was at her side in an instant, gathering her sister into her arms. "I didn't realize. I'm so sorry."

Christina buried her face in Bailey's shoulder and continued to cry, hard, as though she hadn't been able to release her pain until now.

Bailey held her, her heart aching for her sister. She'd been aware that Christina was unhappy, but she hadn't known the extent of her grief. The Campbell boys had seriously gotten under the Farrell girls' skins.

After a while, Christina's sobs quieted, but she kept her head on Bailey's shoulder as she wiped her eyes. "Don't let things go wrong between you and Adam. Promise me, okay?"

"There aren't any *things* between me and Adam," Bailey said quickly. "If he was mad last night because I was with Kyle, it's because he and Kyle have always had it in for each other. If one of them has something, the other wants it. That's all."

Christina's eyes were still wet, but her smile broke through. "You are so dreaming. Adam has a jones for you. He did before he left home, and it's still there."

"Sure, that's why he walks out of a room when I walk in, and hightails it down the road whenever I go to the ranch to work."

"Give him a break. He's hurting, and he's probably touchy about the way he looks now. I bet he doesn't want you to see him beaten-down. Adam's like that."

Bailey had to concede that Adam was self-conscious, and she couldn't blame him. She'd been gun-shy when she'd first returned to Riverbend, wanting to hide from the world for a while. And she hadn't been burned on half her body, hobbling on crutches.

"You're saying I shouldn't let him walk away," Bailey said. "That I should chase his face?"

Christina sat up, shrugging as she reached for her iced tea. "Worked the first time, didn't it?"

Bailey blinked. "Wait. Are you saying I chased him before? I did *not*."

"Oh, come on. You followed him around since you were in grade school. Talked about him constantly too. It was cute, your crush on him." Christina grinned, though tears lingered on her face.

Bailey returned to blushing furiously. "I swear, Christina, you are— you're —"

"Right, and you know it." Christina chuckled. "Tell Kyle you just want to be friends and see what Adam has to offer." She lost her smile. "Seriously, Bailey. Don't let a chance of happiness go. It might not work out, but if you don't try, you'll never know, will you?"

Bailey said nothing as she finished her mimosa. The way her entire body flared to life whenever she saw Adam told her that Christina spoke the truth.

What they'd started all those years ago hadn't ever finished. She and Adam had hugged, said good-bye, and pretended it was better that they parted friends and didn't wait for each other. But it *had* mattered. Maybe Bailey wouldn't have been blinded to Lawrence's shortcomings if she hadn't been trying so hard to forget about Adam.

Christina was right. What the hell? If Bailey talked to Adam, told him how she felt, and not let him simply disappear back into his movie life, what was the worst that could happen?

Except her walking away from a job she loved because it would be too awkward with him there, or her heart shattering into pieces when he left for California again.

Sure. No downside at all.

Bailey chased the last drop of mimosa out of the glass and stared morosely at the empty flute.

\*\*

"What the fuck? What the total *fuck*?"

Adam glared down at the letter, pages and pages of it, but the first couple of paragraphs gave him the gist.

He was being sued for his part in the accident that had lost Dawson his life.

"Son of a fucking *bitch*!"

"Hey," a soft voice said. "You all right?"

Perfect. "Bailey. Now is *not* a good time."

Bailey remained in the outline of the open front door, holding the screen door as she peered inside.

No one else was around. Olivia had gone down to the barn with Tyler and Grant, Ross was at work, and Carter was off doing whatever the hell he was off doing.

Monday afternoon warmth poured in through the door as Adam stood with the mail he'd just opened. Special delivery—he'd had to sign for it, which he had without thinking anything about it.

"What's wrong?" Bailey took a step inside, releasing the screen door, which banged closed behind her.

"Nothing—just ..."

He couldn't stay calm, couldn't talk. Adam bent the papers in his clenching fists, then hurled them away from him. The sheaf hit the floor and the pages scattered across the carpet.

"Damn, damn, *damn it* ..."

He tried to stride off as he'd always done when he lost his temper, taking him away from others so they wouldn't come under fire of his raw anger.

This time, Adam stepped wrong on his still-healing leg, twisted it, and went down. "*Fucking hell!*" His teeth clenched, and he rocked in pain.

Bailey was there, as she had been last night, cool hands catching him, steadying him. Helping him.

"You okay?" she asked. "Lean on me—we'll get you to the couch."

"Bailey, could you leave me the hell alone!"

Adam heard the roar come out before he could stop it. He wanted Bailey, wanted her with every breath, and all he could do was yell at her.

Bailey's face lost color, but her brows came down. "No. I can't."

Adam tried to get his leg under him, but pain shot through it, and it folded up again. "Shit."

"I *could* leave you in the middle of the floor until someone comes home and finds you," Bailey said, her voice hard. "I *could* kick you right now with my dirty boots. But I won't. Now grab on to me, so I can haul you up."

Adam managed to keep the swear words under his breath as he looped his arm around Bailey's neck.

She pulled him to his feet. His tendons stretched and ached as he and Bailey hobbled the few steps together to the living room sofa and collapsed on it.

Bailey ended up squashed next to him against the sofa's arm, Adam half on top of her. She was a soft landing place. Bailey smelled of wind and sunshine, and Adam wanted to warm himself on her forever.

She struggled to sit upright. Adam didn't want to let her. He remained heavy on her, groaning a little as she pushed at him.

*Poor Adam, he can't move — you'll just have to stay here and let me lie on you.*

"Adam, come *on*."

Adam groaned louder. His anger was still there, and underneath it a blackness that was going to swallow him, but he'd push it aside for the goodness of Bailey.

"You're faking it. Get off me, you big lump." Bailey gave him a shove, and Adam finally heaved himself upright.

"Hey, stop pushing. I'm hurt, remember?"

"Yeah, I feel sorry for you. Get over it." Bailey shoved her hair from her eyes, her face pink. "What happened? What are those papers about?" She waved her hand at the crumpled pages on the floor.

Adam dropped against the back of the sofa, resting his head on it and running his hands through this hair. "They want to sue me, end my career, take all I've got."

"*Sue* you? Who does? Why? "

Adam turned his head, his rage flaring then dying away into quiet bleakness. "Dawson's brother and his wife. They don't just want to sue *me*. They want the ranch, our training business, all of it, my mom's share and my brothers' as well as mine. They'll punish all the Campbells to get to me." He looked limply at Bailey, wanting to lose himself in her deep brown eyes. "They want to take away everything we have. All we've worked for. Every last bit of it."

# Chapter Eight

Bailey listened in horror. "Why are they suing *you*?" She itched to fetch the papers, but to do that meant getting off the sofa, where Adam sat so warmly next to her. She wouldn't move right now for the world. "It was an accident."

"I don't know." Adam scrubbed his hand over his hair again. "Dawson's brother was always a serious pain in Dawson's ass, and his wife was even worse. Dawson never got along with them. When their parents passed, Dawson inherited most of the money and his dad's big house in Oklahoma. His brother always gave him hell for it—for that, and for going into stunt work." Adam let out a breath. "Mark told me Dawson's brother went after the studio, but the studio has so many lawyers they'll tie the whole thing up for decades. I'm an easier target. Easy to blame me and get some money while he's waiting for a settlement or whatever from the studio."

"But ..." Bailey's brows drew together. She didn't like Adam's haunted look, something darker behind his anger. "I mean why *you*? It wasn't your fault. You were as much a victim as Dawson."

Adam rested his head against the back of the sofa. "That's what you don't get, Bailey. What no one gets. It *was* my fault. I screwed up, and my best friend died."

He closed his eyes, the lines around them tightening. Adam had always believed that men shouldn't cry — or if they did, at least make sure they were a hell of a long way from anyone. He didn't cry now. But his anguish rang loud and clear, even if he didn't make a sound.

"It can't have been your fault. There was an investigation, wasn't there? Accident reports?" Bailey spoke confidently as she laid her hand on his shoulder.

She got lost a moment in the steel hardness of his muscles under her fingers, the amazing strength his injuries hadn't drained. Bailey sat on his left side, where all the scars showed on his face, ruining the male perfection that had been Adam. Even so, his vitality blazed through. Rather than being a disfigurement, the scars had become a part of him and what he was.

Adam opened his eyes, his fury returning. "Yeah, the report said the truck's engine stalled and the steering wheel jammed, spinning the truck out of control. But we would have found problems like that if we'd been more careful. But the director was rushing, the shot had to be finished that day — too expensive to carry over another day — and Dawson was pushing for it. There were new people on the set—people I didn't know. I was the one to decide whether to run it or not, and I got talked into going through with it. We should have waited, rechecked the setup, sent his truck back to maintenance, to hell with the schedule. All I had to do was say no, and Dawson would still be alive."

It hurt him, hurt him deeply. Bailey realized where his touchiness had come from these past weeks, more than from just his injury. He'd been going over and over the accident in his head, reliving his decision, second-guessing what he should have done. He'd been picturing what would have happened if he'd argued, stood his ground, not let people talk him into doing what he knew would be dangerous. Whether he could have prevented the accident or not didn't matter. Adam believed himself responsible.

He'd been bottling this up inside him, keeping it silent all these weeks, while his brothers had teased him, and she'd chided him.

"Adam, I'm so sorry," Bailey said in a near-whisper.

She slid her hand from his shoulder and laid her head there instead. Adam's skin was hot beneath his shirt—Bailey could feel his chest lift with his breath, the thrum-thrum of his pulse in his throat.

Then his fingers were cupping her cheek, lifting her face to his. Adam's blue eyes filled her vision, an inch or so from hers.

"You're feeling sorry for me again." His voice was low, an irritated growl.

"Yes." Bailey refused to move, to stammer, to apologize. She was finished being the shy girl. She had a lot to give, and a lot to offer. She wasn't going anywhere.

Adam's mouth set into a grim line. "Tell me the truth. Are you with Kyle?"

Bailey resisted the urge to answer, *No, I'm with you,* but she knew what he meant. "If you're asking whether we're a couple, no," she said. "We've been out a few times, but not often, and we agreed it's not exclusive. We're keeping it light."

Adam didn't seem to hear anything past *no.* "I'm one to take what I want. But I won't take what isn't mine."

"No?" Bailey asked in surprise. "I thought you and Kyle fought over everything."

"Not when it's important."

His gaze unnerved her, his eyes lake blue with lighter blue flecks. "And this is important?"

Adam's answering smile pierced her to the bone. "Yes."

"Adam ..." There she went. Blushing, stammering. *I'm one to take what I want.* "What are you saying you want?"

"You." His grin widened. "What did you think? Brussels sprouts?"

Bailey cleared her throat, tried to sit up—she couldn't—and said, "So, when were you going to bother to tell me? You've been home five weeks."

"Five weeks, three days, and a couple of hours," Adam said. "I was going to tell you when I was good and ready."

"And you're ready right now?"

Adam traced her cheek with a finger that shook, but not with fear. "Right now, I'm mad as hell, hurting all over, and just found out I'm going to lose everything I care about. This is as good a time as any."

In spite of his rage, his fingers were firm, his touch strong, filling Bailey with fire. "You won't lose everything," she said. She wouldn't let that happen.

Adam didn't appear to hear her. "Just so you know, I'm not good with the romantic stuff. I don't know the right things to say. I only know that you're beautiful, and it's ripping me up inside not having you." His fingers moved on her face, his touch electric. "I'm beat up and broken, and scared of everything that's going to come next, but just sitting here with you is making me better. So I'm going to hold on, all right? When you want me to let go and leave you alone, you tell me, but not … Not right now."

"Not right now," Bailey whispered, her heart full—then she laced one hand behind his neck and pulled him into the kiss she'd been imagining since she'd seen him stagger to the porch the night he came home.

Adam stilled, his hand on her face quieting. The next moment, he came down to her with hard need, kissing her back, seeking, taking.

This wasn't the kiss of a man defeated, or ruined. This was a man who'd gone into the world with nothing, faced it, succeeded. Would face it again.

Right now, he needed a break. He needed to kiss her.

Their bodies moved together, his grip tightening, securing her against him with no intention of releasing her.

Bailey was aware of nothing but Adam. His breath on her skin. His mouth, firm and hot. His hand on her back, holding her in place.

Adam bit down on her lower lip, the heat of that washing her clean. Bailey made a noise in her throat and he curved over her, pushing her against the arm of the sofa.

Her shirt loosened, Adam's hands sliding under the fabric, heat in the sun-warmed room. Adam glided his touch around her back to her bra, easily finding the catch. He unhooked the bra as he deepened his kiss, pushing it aside to take his palms to the swell of her breasts.

Bailey wanted to gasp, groan, make any kind of noise as Adam caressed her. His thumbs found her nipples, which were already firm little points, stirring fire deep inside her.

She arched into him and slid her hands down his back, craving his touch.

Adam eased away from the kiss, still cradling her breasts in his work-roughened hands. Bailey's shirt had lifted high, and his gaze dropped to her bareness, exposed in sunlight.

"You're even more beautiful," he said, triumph in his eyes. "I knew you would be."

For a man who claimed he didn't know the right things to say, Adam was melting her heart.

On Adam's part, his pulse was pounding fast, the heat inside him making him dizzy. Maybe his head wasn't all the way healed from the beating it had taken in the accident, or maybe it was just Bailey leaning back on the couch, her dark eyes half closed, her hair a mess, her shirt up, revealing to him how gorgeous she'd become. Her breasts were plump, filled out from what he remembered, her large nipples tight and dark.

She'd look even better out of her dusty work clothes and wrapped in sheets—better still, bare on top of his bed.

She'd always been sexy without knowing it. Adam had met plenty of women who were aware of their own looks, and what those looks could get them. It made them grasping and cold, with nothing behind their sultriness but hard greed.

Bailey, on the other hand, had no idea she was beautiful. She'd called herself a frumpy nerd, and those idiots she'd taken up with in Austin probably hadn't corrected her. Her stupid husband hadn't appreciated what he'd had. Only a moron would give up Bailey, didn't matter what other woman walked past.

Adam wanted to tell her all kinds of things—*I missed you; I thought about you every day; When I saw you here, everything started to come together again.*

Coherent speech was beyond him, though, which right now didn't really matter.

Bailey let out a gentle sigh, her body moving under his touch. Adam's heart beat faster, his cock so hard it was aching. He needed her hand on it, or her lips, her tongue …

*Damn,* but he shouldn't think of things like that. Adam leaned down, ignoring the twinge in his bad leg, and licked between her breasts.

Her soft gasp had him growing even harder. Bailey laced her fingers through his hair and pulled him to her, encouraging him.

Adam licked again, moving to trace her nipple with his tongue, teasing the point before he closed his mouth over it.

He liked the noises she made. The little moan as he suckled her, the half squeal as he gently bit the tip of her nipple. Adam had known women who'd faked every feeling; Bailey showed nothing but honesty.

Adam knew that if he worked his way inside her jeans he'd find her wet, her honey beckoning his fingers and his mouth. The thought of Bailey spread while he licked her, tasting every bit of her, made his wild need ramp high.

It had been way, way too long since he'd had any sex. He was in danger of coming right there, without undressing, like a crazed teenager.

But with Bailey, Adam would be forever young, and it would be forever new.

"Ah…" The one syllable cut into the room, Grant's drawl unmistakable.

Bailey jerked in alarm and tried to squirm away, but Adam grabbed her and held her back. "Wait. It's only Grant."

Bailey subsided, wide-eyed as Adam drew her shirt down to hide her nakedness. He took his time lifting away from her, turning to his brother who stood just inside the front door, hat in hand, staring awkwardly at the ceiling.

"What?" Adam asked him.

Grant took a swift glance at Bailey, saw she was covered, and relaxed slightly. "Yeah, it's only Grant, *right now*," he said. "The rest of the pack are heading up the hill, with Faith. It's a half day at her school.

Carter picked her up, and they're coming in to make a big lunch."

"Oh, God." Bailey scrambled up, smoothing her shirt back into place, her face red. "Grant ..."

Grant gave her a wink. "Hey, I can keep a secret. And it's a *good* secret. Adam and Bailey, back together. As it should be."

"We're not ..." Bailey huffed, regaining some of her dignity. "This was just ..."

"Adam groping you? Yep, I saw." Grant grinned. "If you're not back together, then you're friends with benefits. But even friends with benefits don't do it on a couch by the front door with a ton of people about to walk in."

Adam heaved himself from the sofa and stood at Bailey's shoulder. "Leave her alone. And keep your mouth shut."

"Don't I always?" Grant made a show of zipping his lips, locking them, throwing away the key.

"No, you don't. You gossip like a girl." Adam put his arm around Bailey. "Don't embarrass her."

She pulled away, anger in her eyes. "He can't embarrass me any more than I already am. I'll see you guys later."

Adam couldn't believe how empty he felt as Bailey left the circle of his arm, determined to go. If Adam opened his mouth, he'd call after her, beg her not to leave, dignity and self-reliance gone to hell.

Grant spoke for him. "Stay to lunch, Bailey. Faith will want to see you."

Bailey's face reddened more. "No—I'll grab lunch somewhere. You all have a lot to talk about."

She looked pointedly at the papers still scattered across the floor. *Damn it.* Adam would need to explain what was going on, something he didn't look forward to. He'd hoped Bailey would remain and help him break this news.

But no, there she went, out the door. Grant didn't stand in her way, didn't try to stop her.

Adam went out after her, and Grant didn't stand in his way either. Adam's bad leg slowed him down, but he caught her at the bottom of the porch stairs.

"Bailey, don't." He closed his hand over her wrist, holding her too tightly. "Grant will keep his mouth shut. He likes you."

"It's not that," Bailey said. Well, her mouth said that. Her eyes told him she was embarrassed and ashamed, and didn't want to face the horde of Campbells after Adam had been feeling her up. "You have to tell them about the lawsuit and what it means. That's family stuff. I shouldn't be here for that."

*You're family*, Adam wanted to say, but at that moment Faith saw Bailey and came bouncing toward her.

Bailey jerked from Adam's hold. She moved to Faith with a swift stride, intercepting her. Adam heard the little girl's disappointment when Bailey told her she had to go. Carter gave Adam a puzzled frown as he neared, but fortunately didn't ask questions.

Adam let Bailey go—for now. Not much he could do, not with his family flowing up from the drive to the house.

He watched Bailey get into her small pickup and slam the door, not looking at him or anyone else as she started it up. Faith waved to her, and Bailey flashed a smile at the girl and waved back. Then

Bailey pulled out, gravel spraying as she punched the gas too hard and the tires spun.

She drove off in a big hurry down the long dirt lane, the dust in her wake dissipating in the warm, blue sky.

\*\*

Bailey's hands were sweating on the steering wheel, her breath coming so fast it hurt, but she realized she needed to slow down and take it easy. Wouldn't help if she wrecked her truck or hit someone else—or was pulled over for speeding by Deputy Ross Campbell. That would make the day perfect.

Her wrists, neck, breasts, all held bands of fire where Adam had touched her. Her mouth was raw, tender, everything a reminder of him and how much she wanted him.

If Grant hadn't come in … It was a good thing he had. The entire family would have found Adam with his hands up Bailey's shirt, her nipple in his mouth. They'd have found a shotgun and made Adam propose.

Worse, they'd have laughed. Adam didn't need to be laughed at right now. He needed … well, Bailey wasn't sure what, but teasing him for losing control wasn't it.

She took her foot from the gas and glided down the road at an even speed, slowing to the requisite thirty-five when she hit the town limits. *Welcome to Riverbend,* the sign the town council had raised said. *Home of the Friendliest People in Texas.*

Bailey had intended to head to her house and recover her equilibrium, but her truck's fuel gage showed the tank was empty. She sighed and pulled into Riverbend's one gas station.

The family who owned the station had also built the restaurant next door, turning the corner into one of the most popular in town. Breakfast time on weekends saw the place packed, Mrs. Ward's biscuits and gravy the best in the county.

Bailey pulled in next to the pumps and got out, her movements wooden. She'd fuel up, go home to her cozy little house, sit down, and try to cool off. Later she'd have to go back to the Campbell's ranch—she was helping Grant and Tyler work up a new act for the Fall Festival. She couldn't let them down because their brother had kissed her.

She'd have to face Adam again, look into his eyes, remembering the feeling of his mouth on hers, his hands hot under her breasts. When they'd been younger, and Adam had made love to her, he'd been all smiles and energy—now he had the slow assuredness of experience, knowing how to draw a woman into passion …

"Bailey."

Bailey jumped, the gas nozzle in her hand, and nearly splashed herself with fuel. She quickly shoved the nozzle into her tank and locked it in place.

She straightened up, facing Kyle Malory, hoping Adam hadn't left actual marks on her skin. "Hey, Kyle. How are you?"

Kyle grinned, his easy handsomeness a contrast to Adam's ruined face and intense eyes. "'Bout the same as last time you saw me. Want to grab a drink when you're done tonight?"

"Um …" *Tell me the truth. Are you with Kyle?* Adam's voice rang in her head. She remembered the hard, almost desperate look in his eyes when he'd asked the question.

"Not tonight," Bailey said quickly to Kyle. "I'm going to be working my butt off this afternoon, and I plan to fall asleep as soon as I'm home."

Kyle shrugged, unworried. "Tomorrow then."

He looked certain that she'd pick a night, and they'd make a date. Another evening of beers and pool, followed by Kyle kissing her good-night in his truck, confident that she'd invite him inside; if not tonight, then one of these nights.

"No, sorry, I'm doing something with Christina tomorrow night."

He nodded, still unconcerned. "Weekdays are crazy. How about I pick you up on Saturday? About nine? Give us both a chance to wash the horse sweat off us."

*"Kyle."*

The firm note in her voice made him frown, his green eyes narrowing. Every girl in town envied Bailey the scrutiny of those brilliant emerald eyes.

Kyle looked her up and down with them now. "What's wrong? I like your company, Bailey. Pick a time, and tell me. I'm not a pushy guy."

Bailey gave a short laugh. "Yes, you are. But that's not why. It's not—"

"Crap on a crutch." Kyle held his hand straight out. "Stop right there. Are you about to say *It's not you, it's me?*"

"Well, it isn't you." Bailey folded her arms, wanting to shiver, even though the late September sun was plenty warm. "I'm just not ready to be serious again."

"Serious?" Kyle stared at her. "There's nothing serious. We go to the bar, we talk and have fun. We haven't even gone to bed. I haven't had a relationship this *not*-serious in a long time. I didn't think I was pushing you."

"You're not. That's why I'm saying it's me. I need more time."

Kyle studied her for a while, sunlight glittering in his eyes. Then his brows came together, anger sparking at last.

"Bailey, you lying shit," he said. "I never knew you had it in you."

# Chapter Nine

"What?" Bailey's temper rose. "Watch who you're calling a shit. What am I lying about?"

"This I'm-not-ready-to-get-serious crap you're trying to pull on me." Kyle's gaze was sharp, his face dark with anger. "Has nothing to do with waiting until you're ready, does it? It's Adam, right? I saw how you were with him during the pool game Saturday night. You looked like you wanted to crawl all over him."

Bailey drew herself up. "I did not. I was out with you. I don't do that." Certainly not after she'd been on the receiving end of what being cheated on felt like. Which was why she would not go out with Kyle again. Not while Adam had possession of her every thought.

"You were all over him *in here*." Kyle tapped the side of his forehead. "What the hell do you see in him? Adam Campbell is so fucking full of himself. Deserted his family for the fame of Hollywood, and look what it got him? Banged up and half dead, and everyone feels sorry for him, including you. But don't fool yourself." He folded his arms, closing himself off. "He won't care about you, Bailey. He only wants to win. Me and him have been scrapping since we were six, and I've learned a thing or two about Adam. He'll do anything to get what he wants, but that don't mean he wants it forever. I've heard the stories of what he did out in L.A. — the parties with escorts, the women he dates and drops like they were nothing. Women are all over him, but he takes the ones he wants, uses them, and he's done."

His speech stabbed uncertainty through her, which only made Bailey angrier. "How do you know?" she snapped. "You've never been to L.A., and I doubt he texts you about his conquests."

Kyle gave her a patient look. "Because he tells Grant. Grant told Christina everything when they were together, Christina is good friends with my sisters, and they told me. Can't keep a secret in a small town, even if you're a thousand miles away from it."

Bailey's face warmed. She knew stories like that would get around — she'd been oblivious of them in her closed-off life in Austin — but she also knew they got exaggerated.

"I'm sure there are great stories about him," she said. "Told over and over until there's a little bit of truth left, but not much."

"Sweetheart, if Adam had had a long-term relationship with a woman, any woman, you'd have known it. Everyone in town would have told you, even when you were living with your high-tech city friends. Look around — do you see him married with kiddies? Bringing home a steady girlfriend to meet the family? Trust me, as soon as Adam feels better, he'll be running right back to his nonstop-action life, and you'll be just another conquest. Don't let him do that do to you."

"I am *not* a conquest." Bailey drew a sharp breath, unable to banish Adam's dark voice saying *I'm one to take what I want.* "It doesn't matter. I meant it when I said I didn't need anything serious. With you *or* with him."

Kyle studied her a moment longer, then he gave a little nod, as though deciding something. "What's sad is you really believe that. Tell you what—you do what you think you have to. When Adam breaks your heart and stomps all over it, then hightails it back to L.A., you give me a call. If I'm not still pissed off at you, we might go for beers again. Okay?"

Bailey let out a sigh. "Kyle, I'm sorry …"

"Don't be sorry, babe." Kyle slapped on the black cowboy hat he'd taken off to talk to her. "Just be careful. You've been burned, and you're vulnerable. Remember that. See you round, Bailey. Give my best to your sister." He gave her a polite nod and stalked off toward his truck he'd left in front of the convenience store.

The pump had long since shut off, Bailey's tank filled. She jerked the nozzle from the tank and hung it up, taking the receipt from the automated machine.

Kyle's truck roared to life as she closed up her gas tank. In spite of his anger at her, he didn't peel out or drive recklessly. He calmly pulled out into the road, waiting for one car to pass before he did. He didn't turn his head to look at Bailey—his hat pointed straight ahead as he drove off into the afternoon sunshine.

Bailey got into her truck but sat motionlessly in the driver's seat for a long time. Adam's touch had fired her, imprinting himself on her. Kyle's words cut cold through that.

Of course Bailey hadn't expected Adam to be a saint, and they hadn't had any kind of understanding when he'd left. They'd parted as friends only, no commitments—they'd both known they wouldn't be able to keep any promises. Their lives would be too different, too far apart.

Adam and Bailey were older now, both damaged by life, both starting again. Could Kyle not see that? Or could Kyle see the truth, because he had a better perspective, not being too close to either of them?

No, Bailey decided. Kyle was Adam's rival and always would be. Kyle would do everything he could to keep Adam from having what he wanted; they'd always been at odds.

Bailey sat in her truck so long as her thoughts churned that one of the guys who worked at the station came over to her.

"Can I help you with anything, Miss Farrell?" he asked, peering in through her open window. He was a nice kid, about eighteen—he called any woman over twenty-one *Miss*, regardless of their marital status.

"No, I'm fine," Bailey said, smiling up at his scruffy face. "I was just daydreaming."

"Hey, if you're hungry, Mrs. Ward's bringing in the first harvest pies of the season. Take one home."

"Thanks, I might." Bailey started her truck and drove slowly across the parking lot toward the restaurant. Still troubled, she did go inside and buy a pie to take home. She'd have a slice for lunch and take it to the Campbells' with her this afternoon. They'd eat every crumb of it before dinner. Guaranteed.

** **

Adam's family took the news of the lawsuit surprisingly well. Or, not so surprisingly. They were angry but ready to fight, all of them behind him. Adam looked up and down the dining-room table, warming at the determination on their faces.

"I know a lot of lawyers," Carter said when Adam finished. "Want me to call one?"

"No, I have lawyers," Adam said. "But I'll keep it in mind. Who knows if I might need the extra help?"

Carter had hired a private detective and lawyers when Faith's mother had dumped her then disappeared. He'd wanted to find the woman and try to make her care about the daughter she'd abandoned. Didn't work. After a time, Carter had decided Faith was better off staying with him and stopped trying.

"Thanks, Carter," Adam said, touched. Carter rarely liked to mention, even indirectly, his problems with Faith's mother.

Carter gave him a steady look. "You're a dickhead, but you're my brother."

"Now, boys," Olivia said, folding her tanned arms on her placemat. "No name calling at the table. We're behind you, Adam. You've worked too hard to have this happen to you. It wasn't your fault."

Adam didn't correct her. He didn't feel right talking about it with anyone but Bailey. "This doesn't only affect me," he said. "They want to shut the whole business down."

"We'll fight it," Tyler said, reaching for another helping of potato salad. "Don't you worry, Adam. Nothing can stop Campbells, once they team up."

"And Sullivans," Faith said. "Don't forget us."

"Like I could." Tyler sent his niece a grin.

His family looked concerned, but not unduly worried. Adam was plenty worried, but he liked that they had his back. It was a good feeling.

He carried that feeling with him, as well as the memory of Bailey's soft lips, the taste of her breast filling his mouth, all the way through the afternoon to the bar that night.

Grant was with him, the two of them not talking much over the music. Grant had come because Christina had the night off, probably out with Ray Malory. What the hell did Bailey and her sister see in those two?

Kyle Malory made the night worse by coming up to the bar and leaning on it next to Adam. He ordered his favorite beer from the pretty female bartender, who responded to his smile with a swift one of her own.

He winked at her when he took his beer, and she said, "Oh, come on, Kyle, quit," before turning away to another customer, leaving Kyle with Adam.

Over the blast of the music, Kyle said to Adam, "I'm going to kick your ass, Campbell."

Grant, hearing, craned to look around Adam. "Picking on a man when he's down, are you? Just like a Malory."

Kyle scowled at him. "This is between me and Adam. You coming outside?" he asked Adam.

Adam closed his hand around his beer bottle. "Not going anywhere with you until you tell me what the hell you're talking about. If this is about the pool game, I won that fair and square."

"I don't give a shit about the pool game. This is about Bailey."

Adam was off his seat before Kyle's last syllable was swallowed by the thumping beat of the latest country-rock band. He had his hand on Kyle's shoulder, feeling Kyle quivering with anger under his palm, and steered the other man around the tables and outside.

# Chapter Ten

The parking lot had plenty of people in it, from those who wanted to talk away from the music to couples entwined in the shadows. No alcohol was allowed beyond a certain point, and the far side of the parking lot was deserted.

Adam set his beer on the rim of a pickup bed. He knew the guy standing there kissing his wife, and said, "Watch that for me, Mike," before walking with Kyle, who'd shaken off his hold, to the empty side of the lot.

Grant was right behind Adam, and Carter, who'd seen them go, came after them. One of Kyle's friends, seeing them and scenting trouble, broke off from the group he'd been talking with to come stand beside Kyle.

"I told you," Kyle said, glaring at Grant and Carter as they all stopped in the shadows. "This is between me and Adam."

"And Adam is recovering from one hell of a crash," Grant said. "We're staying."

"I'm fine," Adam said, voice hardening. "I could have kicked Kyle's ass when my leg was still in the splint. I only came out here because I want to hear what he has to say about Bailey. Be really careful what that is, Malory. I'm in a bad mood."

"I'm talking about how you're fucking with her," Kyle said. "The look in her eyes when she spoke about you today almost broke my heart. She's all bent out of shape over you, and you're treating her like a piece of shit."

"She said that?" Adam asked. Is that what Bailey thought? She'd been unhappy when she'd left the ranch, and Adam did not like the idea that he'd made her so. He also didn't like that she'd spilled everything to Kyle. *If* she had. This could be Kyle's bullshit.

"She didn't have to," Kyle was saying. "She was upset when I saw her this afternoon, and I know it was because of you. She'd not one of your dressed-up whores, Campbell. She doesn't understand guys like you."

"What, she understands guys like you?" Adam's anger ran hot. He'd been around pushy shits for years now, and he'd learned to handle them, but Kyle always brought out the worst in him.

"I'm trying to save Bailey some hurting," Kyle said. "You're hurting her, so I'm going to kick your ass for it."

"Good." Adam made a show of rolling up his sleeves. "I'm getting bored sitting around with nothing to do. Come on."

Carter, the only one who ever dared get between Adam and something he was after, came around Adam and faced Kyle. "You're not going to hit a man who's been injured as bad as he has," he told Kyle.

"It's all right, baby bro," Adam said. "He'll never see what's coming."

Grant flanked Adam on the other side. "Cool it, Adam. You're not fighting. If he wants to go at it, he can take Carter and me."

Kyle's friend Jack, who was about six feet three with a shaved head and solid, tattooed arms stepped next to Kyle, looking ready to start in.

Kyle made a negating signal. "My beef is with Adam. I'll save the fight until he's better — that's only fair — but this is between me and him. The rest of you can stay out of it. You too, Jack."

Jack said nothing, remaining stoic as always. Jack Hillman was also a friend of Carter's, but he always backed up the Malorys for some reason.

"I agree," Adam said. "No one else involved; no one else gets hurt."

"Exactly," Kyle said. "Only I've thought of something better than a fight. We can punch at each other anytime. I want this to count."

"Sure you do," Adam said, impatient. "Don't chicken out — afraid I'll make you look bad?"

"This will be better than a straight fight," Kyle said, his angry look smoothing into his slick smile. "I want you losing to me in front of more people than your brothers. I want this in front of the entire town."

"All right." Adam was boiling, ready to light into him, but he could be a good sport. "Then everyone can watch me beat the crap out of you."

"Not a fight. A challenge. The Fall Festival is coming up in a couple weeks. We face off in a place we're on equal footing, so to speak." He shot a glance at Adam's healing leg. "The riding arena. I'll be happy just to prove I'm better than the great Hollywood stuntman, but if you want to make it more interesting with a bet ..."

"Are you kidding me?" Adam heard his own voice sounding normal, as though he didn't care. "I ride professionally. That's not a challenge."

"I ride professionally too, dirtbag. I stick to the rodeo circuit while you live in cushy hotel rooms and rehearse every move you make. This is life, not the movies. Out here, it's raw, and real."

Thinking about some of the condemned motel rooms and supply closets he'd had to sleep in at shoots, and the twenty-hour days with no sleep and little food, made Adam want to laugh. Kyle didn't have a clue what he was talking about. The movie life looked glamorous from the outside but was a lot of grungy work on the inside.

Kyle waited, watching, for Adam to agree.

Adam imagined himself jumping up on a horse to easily best Kyle ... and something clenched around his solar plexus. Adam's next breath was hard coming, his throat closing up.

What the hell was wrong with him? He'd done far scarier things than enter a show ring at the Fall Festival. He'd fallen backward off a twenty-story building, hit the corner of his landing bag instead of the middle, broke his foot and his hand and scuffed himself bloody, and still had climbed back up to the roof for another take.

Now the idea of mounting a horse and riding it around, doing the tricks he'd done since the age of four, scared the shit out of him.

The night receded with a rush and a roar. Adam heard the crackling of fire, the shouting, the horrified yells, the screech and groan of metal, the popping sound of exploding brick. Flames filled his vision.

They receded slightly to show him Dawson, a tall man who hadn't been considered very good-looking, but the ladies had loved him. Dawson had been a heavy partier, up for anything, but always ready to roll in the mornings. He'd had a warm laugh and a deep compassion that Adam hadn't ever found in anyone else, except Bailey.

Adam saw Dawson's smile now, heard his drawl. Dawson was from Tulsa, and Adam, a good Texas boy, was supposed to despise him for being an Okie, but he never could.

"Don't you worry none," Dawson had said on his last day, giving Adam his infectious grin, when Adam had voiced his concerns about the stunt. "We'll be okay. We've done this hundreds of times."

"Not this rushed. They're cutting corners."

Dawson's grin widened. "You worry too much. Let's show 'em how it's done."

Dawson had waved from the truck when he'd been ready to go. He'd smiled at Adam again, just before everything had spun out of control, and Dawson had been engulfed in flames …

Adam couldn't breathe. Darkness was pulsing around him, consumed by fire.

He had to be dreaming he was standing in the parking lot of Riverbend's bar, surrounded by his brothers and Jack, facing Kyle, who waited, smug, for his answer.

Adam viewed the scene as though from somewhere beyond, watching himself stick out his hand and take Kyle's sunburned one. "You got yourself a challenge," he heard himself say.

Kyle clamped down on Adam's hand, but even the familiar handshake, with each of them trying to out-grip the other, didn't snap Adam out of his daze.

"Good, that's settled," Grant said, sounding relieved. "Can I go have a beer now? Kyle, you're buying."

"Sure," Kyle said, finally releasing Adam. "A round for everyone, on me."

Jack grinned and led the way, Grant and Kyle following.

Carter was the only one who didn't relax. He watched Adam closely as usual, waiting to see what he'd do.

Adam couldn't go tamely back into the bar, especially not with Kyle playing host. He couldn't go home either, where his mother and Faith would ask why he was back so early, and was everything all right?

He walked away, his emotions in turmoil. He strode as fast as he could, hoping the flames and the darkness would recede if he walked swiftly enough, but they didn't.

Carter caught up to him, gravel crunching under his boots. "Want me to drive you somewhere?" he asked.

"No." Again Adam watched himself from afar, unable to feel himself doing anything. Reminded him of when he'd flatlined—a dead man walking.

Carter kept stride with him. "Where the hell are you going? If I lose you, Mom will kill me."

Adam swung on him, some of the darkness receding as his anger surged. "Will you leave me the fuck alone?"

"No." Carter remained stubbornly with him, the untamed boy he'd been now a not-quite-tamed man. "Tell me where you're going, and I'll get out of your face."

Adam told him. It wasn't far; he could make it on foot. He knew exactly where his destination was, though he'd never been there before.

Carter scowled. Indecision warred on his hard face, but finally, he nodded. "You need me, you call, all right? You got your cell phone?"

Adam gave him an irritated look. "You know, you and Grant fuss like old men. I'll be fine."

Carter didn't believe him, but at least he fell silent. He watched as Adam walked away, but he didn't follow.

Thank God Mom had chosen Carter to look out for him tonight. Grant, Tyler, or Ross would never have let Adam do what he needed to.

The small houses in an older corner of the town had been falling-down wrecks when he'd been a kid, but in the last decade or so, when people had started wanting small-town life again—though not too far from the big cities—these old houses had been bought and renovated, the area gentrified.

Number 5 was painted a dark brown-red with crisp white trim. It was a shotgun house, meaning it had a door and one window in front, with the rooms placed one behind the other with no hallways—the doors from room to room were all on the same side of the house. *Shotgun* because, in theory, a man could fire a gun through the front door and, if all doors in the house were open, the slug would go straight out the back door without hitting anything in between.

A little porch fronted the house, with two steps leading up to its wooden floor. A porch light was on, highlighting the screen door and the dark brown door behind it. The front window glowed with light, and Adam heard a TV going.

The roar of fire finally started to fade as he raised his hand and knocked. He saw Dawson, surrounded by flame, grinning at him again. *Can't fault your taste, Campbell.*

Then he was gone, replaced by Bailey, who yanked open the front door and stared through the screen. "Adam?"

"Hey," Adam said.

Bailey pushed open the screen door and took a step to him, her brows drawing together. She looked so good, in a tight black shirt with a little satin bow on the neckline, her hair loose, her brown eyes full of concern.

Dignity went to hell. Adam grabbed her hand and hung on. "Bailey," he said, barely able to form the words. "For God's sake, you've got to help me."

# Chapter Eleven

Bailey couldn't quite believe that Adam sat in her living room, on the center cushion of her sofa, leaning on his knees, his head bowed. He'd staggered past her when she'd let him in, ending up on the couch, growling at her to close the door and not let anyone see him.

Bailey locked up then pulled heavy drapes over her living room window's lace curtains. "Adam?"

He didn't respond. He stared down at her carpet, hands dangling between his knees, not moving, not speaking. Lamplight burnished his hair, bringing out the light streaks among the darker strands.

Bailey shoved her small coffee table out of the way and sank onto the sofa next to him. She put her hand on his back and found it moving a little. Not the shaking of a man crying, but of a man shivering and unable to stop.

"You okay?" Bailey caressed Adam's back, his muscles hard beneath her hand, and tried to look into his face. "What did you want me to help you with?"

Adam scrubbed one hand over his face, then his hair. He rubbed his hair again, over and over, until finally he sprang to his feet with a snarl.

"Everything. I need your help with *everything!* This is all so ... Ah, damn it. Fucked to hell."

"You mean the lawsuit?"

Adam's hands came down to his sides, rigid in fists. His short hair was a mess, scars white on his red face, eyes glittering.

He was a man going wild and trying not to. Adam had never contained himself, rushing after whatever he wanted, doing whatever he pleased, and always coming out on top.

His world had changed, life had changed, and he didn't know how to face it.

"Screw the lawsuit. I don't know what the hell's wrong with me, Bailey. I used to be fearless—I'd do anything. I've been thrown out of helicopters, crashed cars and motorcycles, jumped from galloping horses and out of windows, rappelled down buildings and climbed back up them. No matter how hurt I was, no matter how dangerous, I got up and did it again. And now ..." Adam stopped, staring at her as though seeing her and seeing through her at the same time. "Shit, I don't want you to know this."

He swung away, heading purposefully to the front door. Bailey left the sofa and got ahead of him, putting her back against the doorframe.

"No." She placed her hands on his chest. Adam halted, but impatiently, his look angry. "Whatever you tell me will never go beyond this room," Bailey said. "You know that. You asked me to help you." She flattened her palms against him, soaking in the warmth from his T-shirt. "So let me help you."

Adam stared at her a moment longer, the anguish in his eyes fierce. Emitting another growl, he closed the space between them, crushing her between him and the door.

"Stop," he said savagely. "Stop being so ... *you*."

And he kissed her.

Bailey felt the change in him as soon as their mouths met. The man furiously angry became a man aroused. Adam's fists relaxed so his fingers could furrow her hair, and his mouth opened hers. His body softened, giving instead of taking, sharing instead of demanding.

Bailey curled her hands on his back, digging into his shirt, starting to tug it upward as he kissed her. He'd bared her on the sofa this morning; now she wanted to see him.

Adam deepened the kiss, arms going around her, lifting her against the door. He hooked one hand under her hip, drawing her leg up, making it curve around him.

Bailey hung on to him with pleasure. She pulled him closer with her calf on his thigh, the position digging his rigid hardness against her. Her bedroom was behind the door on the other side of the living room. She'd been picturing Adam in there—as much as she tried not to—since he'd come home.

Adam pushed her shirt upward from the back, making a noise of satisfaction when he found she'd already removed her bra. He released her to pull the shirt off over her head, then helped her pull off his.

Maybe the bedroom wasn't necessary. Adam lifted her again, winding both her legs around him this time, her breasts against his bare chest.

His next kiss left her no doubt what he was going to do. No playing, no feeling her up for the fun of it. He meant to take this all the way.

Did Bailey try to fight him off? Tell him to go? Grow offended that he assumed she'd be willing?

Nope. Bailey's heart thumped with excitement and anticipation. It had been a long time since she'd had sex—a *long* time—and she was out of practice. But then, Adam would know exactly what to do.

He unbuttoned and unzipped Bailey's jeans, jerking them open as she clung to him. Warm fingers pushed them down, slid under the waistband of her panties. He unwound her legs from him and pushed her jeans and underwear from her hips. Bailey was already in her stocking feet, no worry about shoes as her jeans slid to the floor.

Now she was naked, in her socks, her back meeting the door one more time, Adam pushing her there.

"Stop me," he said, voice harsh.

"Wha ... ?"

"You've got to stop me." Adam's blue eyes were tight. "Because I won't be able to stop myself."

Bailey remembered Kyle's warning about Adam and women—*He takes the ones he wants, uses them, and he's done.*

Kyle meant that Adam would sate himself on Bailey, and when he felt better, he'd leave town and never see her again.

*Stop me.*

The fury in Adam's eyes was surpassed only by pain, and that, by his need.

Bailey touched his lips. "Don't talk, Adam," she whispered. "Just make love to me."

**

Bailey's gentle words should have snapped some sense into Adam. Instead, they had the opposite effect. He slid his fingers over her smooth flesh and hungrily took her mouth.

The beauty of her stunned him. He hadn't lied when he said he didn't know romantic words. He could only stare, and touch, and savor.

Her back was firm, spine curving to her hips. The shape of her, which she hid beneath work clothes, came to him through his hands. Waist that dipped in but a little soft, thighs hard from riding. Legs supple and strong.

He learned her with his touch as he kissed her lips, moving from her seeking mouth to nip her chin, her cheek. Then back to her mouth, her kisses eager. Her eyes were half closed with the pleasure of it, Bailey holding him in perfect safety.

Adam would never float away into that bad place when he was in Bailey's arms. She wouldn't let him.

He took one step back, breaking the kiss. While Bailey rested her hands on his shoulders, he unbuckled and unzipped his jeans, toeing off his boots so he could slide everything down.

He lost his balance, but Bailey caught him. They toppled together to the wall between door and window, Bailey crushing the heavy drape behind her.

Something inside Adam chided him for wanting to take her standing up in the living room. He should carry her to the bed, make it nice for her. Even their first, fumbling, crazy time way back when had been on his bed, as narrow as it had been.

That day came to him with clarity — bright sunlight pouring through the windows, the bed creaking as they fell to the mattress. The noises of the horses and people working in the stables had come through the open window, and Bailey's smile had warmed him better than the late spring sunshine. Adam had been happy at that moment — the most perfect happiness he'd ever found in his life — and he hadn't even known it.

Bailey smiled at him now, and a taste of that happiness returned.

The sofa was small, but it would have to do. Bailey had strewn it with crocheted afghans, prickly and soft at the same time.

Adam steered Bailey to it, kissing her while he did, leading her in a slow dance. He hooked his arm around her waist and lowered her down to the sofa, coming with her. The couch was too narrow for both of them, and Adam's knee ended up on the floor. Didn't matter — made it easier in some ways.

Bailey was laughing when they finally came together, her leg wrapped around him, her stocking foot brushing his back. She stopped laughing when his cock nudged her opening, but her eyes warmed with welcoming.

Adam held his breath. He touched Bailey's face, the sweetest thing he'd ever seen, and held her gaze as he slid himself inside.

**

Bailey became liquid fire as Adam filled her. He looked straight into her eyes, no turning away, no closing himself to her. He was with *her*, watching *her*.

His brows drew together as she tightened around him, and Bailey's thoughts fluttered and floated away.

Nothing was real but Adam's solid body on hers, his hardness inside her. He held her with steady hands, no more shaking. This was Bailey's Adam, come home.

He started to move. Bailey let out a soft moan, unable to still it. Excitement heated her skin, as did the need to pull him into her. She drew her fingers down to his tight backside, urging him as he began to thrust.

Their position spread her to him, let him slide inside without hindrance. The warm firmness of his cock opened her, making her slick, which let him move even deeper into her.

He knew exactly how to make love to a woman on a slim sofa, how to make the awkwardness of it work. That fact should bother her, but right now, sensation poured in and erased the niggle. It didn't matter. Now was now — the past did not exist.

"Damn, you're beautiful," Adam whispered. "You always have been. I knew." He smiled, proud of himself.

Bailey touched his face and didn't answer. Adam had always been the best-looking man in town, with his blue eyes, handsome face, and sinful smile. His looks were ruined now by the mesh of scars that she smoothed on his cheek. But his eyes were as blue, his smile as cocksure as ever.

His smile faded as he sped his thrusts, need taking over. Smooth and quick, he moved inside her, Bailey made wet by their heat. His breath came faster—so did Bailey's. Sweat trickled across their bodies, melding them. Where they joined was a beautiful ache.

Bailey's hips rose as they kept on. Crazed excitement stirred inside her, blotting out all reason, all awareness but the hard heat of Adam, the fiery wildness at the center of her body. Only that existed, and Adam's blue eyes.

She heard the cries coming from her mouth, a few caught by Adam's kisses, before he bunched his fist beside her, a groan in his throat.

"Aw, damn," he said clearly, and then he was coming.

The sound of their mingled voices spun Bailey into the white-hot madness that was her peak—the two of them made whole for one bright, extraordinary moment.

Bailey wasn't sure when the moment ended, but all was warmth as she crashed back to earth, and the living room sofa, Adam on top of her.

His arms held her safely, his kisses, slow with afterglow, her anchor in the swirling world.

\*\*

A long time later, the street outside quieted, the only noise coming from crickets in Bailey's yard. Adam made himself open his eyes and raise his head from the cushion of Bailey's chest. She was awake, and greeted him with a faint smile.

Something broke in his heart. He'd never seen anything so beautiful. Adam wanted to say her name, but ended up kissing her instead.

He eased back from the kiss and simply enjoyed looking at her. One lock of her sun-kissed brown hair spilled across her forehead. Her lashes were touched with moisture, as though her dark eyes had filled with tears—Bailey's eyes, which Adam had never been able to forget.

He opened his mouth, thinking he should say *something*, but Bailey touched his lips. "If you're going to tell me we shouldn't have done this, don't," she said. "Yes, we should have."

"I don't regret it." Adam didn't, though he knew he'd let go of his control, and had not tried very hard to stop it.

"You'd better not."

"Nah," he said. "I've done stupid things in my life, but this isn't one of them."

Bailey stroked his hair, a nice feeling. Relaxing. Taking all the hurt away.

Any second now, she was going to ask him why he'd pounded on her door begging for her help. He didn't want to talk about it. Not now. And yet, the only one he could talk to these days—about anything—was Bailey.

She didn't ask, however, as though she realized he needed time. Only she would understand that.

Adam closed his eyes, content to stay in this warm cocoon with her. The real world moved on outside, but here, in their haven, nothing could touch them.

A phone rang. Bailey groaned, putting a hand to her head. "Figures."

"Don't get it," Adam said. He lay heavily on top of her, not letting her move. His knee was cramped and rug-burned, but so what?

Bailey started to wriggle out from under him. "If it's my sister, and I don't answer, she'll come over to find out what's wrong."

Adam let out a breath and raised his head. "Families. You gotta love 'em, but at the same time they drive you bat-shit crazy."

Bailey kept squirming, her breasts crushing against his chest, nipples an erotic touch on his skin.

Adam at last let her up. He missed her warmth the second it was gone, but watching her hurry across the room, stark naked, to grab her phone, wasn't bad either.

Bailey dug her cell phone out from under her discarded jeans and answered it. "Christina?" Her expression, which had shown her ready to tell her sister to politely go away, changed abruptly. "What? Slow down. Are you all right? Just tell me what happened."

# Chapter Twelve

Adam watched Bailey's gaze become fixed on nothing, her brow wrinkling as she listened to her sister's rapid words that Adam couldn't hear.

"Just … just sit down and rest. I'll be right there. All right? I have to go, so I can come find you."

A few more calming phrases, and Bailey finally hung up.

Adam was right next to her. He'd not been able to stay away when he saw her agitation, the worried look on her face. Bailey started to move as soon as she clicked off the phone, but Adam caught her in his arms.

"No, hang on, sweetheart. Tell me what happened."

Bailey shoved her hair out of her eyes. "An accident. On the highway. She and Ray … Ray's in the hospital. Christina's all right—she thinks. I have to go."

Accident. Mangled metal, fire, shouting, sirens, Dawson sitting motionless, while Adam couldn't get to him, couldn't move …

Bailey jerked under him, snapping Adam back to the present. Not Dawson, Bailey's sister, the woman she cared most about. Her eyes were wide, her body shaking, her movements frantic.

Adam held her in place. "You're not driving while you're upset like this. I'll take you."

"Take me? But you —" Bailey broke off, biting her lip, her concern for him returning

"Haven't driven since my own accident? I know, but I'm fine. I'm off all my meds. I'm cleared to drive."

"I know, but —"

Adam stopped her words by kissing her gently on the lips. "Bailey, love, if you rush out there in a panic, you'll hurt yourself. Trust me. I got this."

He held on to her as she searched his face, then finally she gave him a nod. Adam let go of her and grabbed his own clothes, thrusting them on, not giving himself time to change his mind.

He finished dressing before Bailey did. Allowed him the pleasure of seeing her bend down for her jeans, easing them on over her hips. She slid her shirt over her bare breasts, shutting them from view, but they moved, unfettered, beneath the fabric.

Adam used Bailey's sexiness to distract him from the ordeal before him, but he knew he had to face it. He held out his hand. "Keys."

Bailey eyed him closely as she dug into her pocket and handed him the keys to her pickup.

Adam didn't let himself think as they left the house for the truck. He hadn't driven since the crash, didn't matter that his doctors had given him the green light on driving. His palms began to sweat, the cool of the evening doing nothing to cut the nervous trickle down his back.

This was for Bailey. She needed him. He had to push aside his panic and help her. Adam knew how to drive and drive well, never letting emotion come between him and operating the machine.

Something deep inside him clenched as he helped Bailey into the small truck's passenger side then walked around and slid into the driver's seat. He sat there, his hands on the steering wheel, feeling the now-familiar fist tighten around his throat, cutting off his air.

*Don't think. Just do.*

Adam slid the key into the ignition and started the truck.

The hum and roar of the engine jarred him, the vibration of the seat adding to his shakes. Bailey was watching him in concern. Damn it, *she* was the one who was supposed to be worried and scared right now, not him.

Bailey reached over and touched his hand. A flood of warmth came to him, and with it, the vision of her hot and moving beneath him, the sound of her delicious cries when she came. Nothing faked — Bailey giving all of herself.

Adam's resolve firmed. He could do this. For Bailey, he could.

He put the truck in gear and pulled out of the driveway.

The only hospital in the area was at the crossroads of two highways about ten miles south of town, on the way to Burnet. There was almost no traffic as he drove out of Riverbend, the one car they passed belonging to Mrs. Ward, heading back to her restaurant.

Bailey kept her hand on Adam's thigh all the way down the back road to the highway. Her pickup was small, a compact black GMC that went with her personality. Cute but tough and got the job done.

They said nothing at all. Bailey sat rigidly, her contact with him as much to calm herself as Adam.

She was the biggest sweetheart in all the world. No other woman would ever be quite like Bailey.

Christina called again as they neared the two-story hospital and outpatient clinic that served most of this part of the county. Adam was familiar with the place, though he could see they'd added a small one-story wing for something-or-other since he'd been gone. He'd come here enough as a kid, both for checkups and after he'd broken bones while riding, or to visit his brothers when they'd broken various things.

He'd seen plenty of doctors and hospitals in his career since then—he liked best the shoots where no one had been injured at all. Lately, of course, Adam had been to too many hospitals, clinics, and physical therapy centers. He was sick of the places.

Bailey directed them to a ward on the second floor. Christina was sitting in the waiting area outside the nurses' station, a bandage wrapped around one wrist, a small piece of gauze taped to her cheek.

Christina flew to her feet and ran at Bailey as soon as she and Adam stepped off the elevator. The two sisters met in a hug, both of them talking at the same time, crying too. Adam stood patiently while they held each other.

"How's Ray?" Bailey was finally able to ask.

"He's in surgery." Tears slid down Christina's face, wetting the gauze. "They think he'll be fine, but this is to make sure. Oh, Bailey, I can't stop crying."

"What happened?" Adam asked her.

Christina's head came up as the rumble of his voice cut across hers. They were the only ones in the waiting area.

"Adam. Didn't know you'd ..."

She broke off, studying Bailey, who started blushing, and then Adam. "Oh," Christina said. "*Oh.*"

"Stop saying *oh*," Bailey said. "Just tell us what happened."

Christina gave them another look, then shook her head. "I don't even know. We were heading to that new steakhouse out by Fredericksburg, the one in the historical mansion. Ray was driving along fine, but an SUV pulled out to pass a semi-truck coming the other way. Didn't even bother to find out if there was someone in the oncoming lane. Ray drove into the ditch, but the SUV clipped us, and we flipped. I don't remember everything, but I was so scared."

Adam had moved to them during her speech, and he put his hand on Christina's shoulder. "But you're all right. That's the main thing to remember."

She was standing up and well, not in a hospital room surrounded by worried faces, with people in scrubs sending a ton of voltage through her body. Nor peeled from the seat of a truck, taken away, body covered, on a stretcher.

Head-ons occurred on two-lane back highways unfortunately and stupidly often. Drivers were drunk, or not paying attention, or over-confident. Adam had found L.A. freeways a snap to drive after Texas back roads.

He tamped down his anger and the deep knots in his stomach. He was here to help Christina and Bailey. *Focus on Bailey.*

"What happened to the other driver?" Bailey was asking.

"Nothing at all," Christina said, tears returning to her voice. "He smashed up his SUV, but he got out, even called the ambulance for us, because I couldn't hold on to my phone. He acted like it was no big deal."

"Tell that to Ray," Bailey said indignantly. "Does Ray's family know?"

Christina nodded. "Yeah, Kyle's on his way, and—"

The ding of the elevator interrupted her. Off came Kyle, face like thunder, and behind him, Grant.

Grant stopped outside the elevator door, looking pole-axed as he stared at Christina. Kyle didn't wait for him, striding past them all to the nurses' station. He gave Adam an irritated, "What are you doing here?" but didn't stop to hear the answer.

Grant remained by the elevator, his face working through different shades of red. Christina stared back at him, as transfixed as he was.

Adam knew that what had been between his brother and Bailey's sister had been powerful. They'd had fights—he'd witnessed several—that were loud and passionate. Their make-up sex had apparently been just as passionate.

Now they were looking at each other as though Adam and Bailey, the hospital, and the nurses ten feet away, didn't exist.

Adam leaned to Bailey. "Let's get some coffee."

"No." Christina dug her fingers into Bailey's arm. "Bailey, stay."

Bailey shot a look at Adam. Adam understood, though he wasn't happy. But he realized that the last thing Christina needed while she was banged up and upset was a confrontation with her ex.

Adam squeezed Bailey's hand as he handed her back her keys. He wanted to lean down and kiss her good-bye, but he knew that if he did, news of the kiss would be all over town by tomorrow. Might be anyway, because Christina had figured out that he'd been with Bailey, and not in a just-friends way, when she'd called. The soap opera of Riverbend ground on.

Adam broke away from Bailey — not an easy thing to make himself do — and went to his brother.

"Come on," he said under his breath. A touch of the elevator button had the door open. Adam pushed Grant in with one hand. The door closed, shutting out Bailey, her warmth, and the sweet hint of afterglow in her eyes.

"Is she all right?" Grant was at Adam's shoulder in the small elevator. "Damn it, Adam, is she all right?"

The elevator lurched downward. Grant's face was gray, lines around his eyes Adam had never seen before.

"Christina?" Adam kept his voice calm. "Yeah, she's fine. It's Ray who got hurt."

"I know; I was with Kyle when he got the call. No one said a word about Christina." Grant's jaw hardened as the slow elevator hit the ground floor and the doors cranked open. "Ray had better pull through, because I'm going to kill him."

Grant strode out and into the night. Adam had to speed up to catch him, his stiff leg protesting. "Christina said it wasn't Ray's fault," Adam said when he reached his brother.

Grant swung around, his eyes flashing with all the rage he'd been bottling up. "Wasn't his fault? Hell yes, it was his fault. It was his fault for having Christina in the car with him at all! What the fuck was he thinking—why can't he leave her the hell alone?"

It might have been a year since Grant's breakup with Christina, but Adam saw that Grant hadn't moved on. The pain in his eyes was as fresh as if he and Christina had split yesterday.

"Sorry, bro." Adam put his hand on Grant's shoulder. They were well into the parking lot, the harsh lights showing the anguish on his brother's face. "You need a drink? Or maybe a coffee? Either way, at home." The last thing Grant needed was to get roaring drunk and thrown out of the bar—the manager would call the cops, and Ross would have to come and arrest his own brother. Ross was always embarrassed when that happened.

Grant wanted to argue, Adam could see, to rage and do something violent. When they'd been younger, he'd have told Adam to go screw himself and taken off. Then Adam would have gone after him and talked him back home. Grant had done the same for Adam, when Adam had needed to let off steam. The two would have gotten into far more trouble than they did if they hadn't had each other's backs.

Grant balled his fists and let out his breath. "Yeah, all right. Let's go home. But I swear to God, Malory's dead meat as soon as he recovers." He started striding for his truck, in which he must have driven Kyle here. Kyle would have been as agitated about Ray as Bailey had been for Christina, and Grant would have offered him a lift, worried about Christina and determined to see her.

The two reached the black 250. Grant unlocked it, then he stopped in the act of opening the door. "Wait a sec, what the hell are *you* doing here? Bailey said she was staying home tonight, and you walked away from the bar …"

His words died as he started to put it together. Adam yanked open the door on the passenger side. "Can we go?" he demanded.

"You went to Bailey's." Grant's agitation turned to interest. "You were at Bailey's house when Christina called her. Am I right?"

Adam growled. "Could you mind your own business?"

Grant's grin shone out. "Aw, man, you *were* with her. I bet you weren't watching TV. Look at your face …" He let out a laugh that was loud if strained, and climbed into the truck.

Adam slid onto the passenger seat and slammed the door. "Keep it to yourself, will you? Bailey doesn't need the whole town talking about her."

"Right." Grant gave him another grin, the truck roaring to life. "I'll keep it between you and me." He shook his head, putting the pickup in gear and swinging out of the lot. "This is great, bro. I always knew you and Bailey were meant for each other."

"Yeah, well, let's just get through tonight," Adam said. Grant laughed again, the truck sliding a little as Grant peeled out of the parking lot and headed back to town.

\*\*

Grant knew. Bailey saw it in his big smile when she came in to work the next morning, late and tired, her dreams keeping her up most of the night.

Tyler apparently *didn't* know—he was all sympathy for Christina's accident—but Grant's look spoke louder than words.

He knew. Christina knew. Which meant that, soon, everyone in town would.

Bailey had stayed with Christina until Ray made it out of surgery. He'd be all right, his mom said— she'd arrived at the hospital not much later than Kyle, with Grace Malory trailing her. The other Malory sister, Lucy, lived in Houston now; she'd been on the phone with Grace as they came in.

Kyle wouldn't look at or talk to Bailey, but the rest of the family had been too worried to notice. Once they knew Ray would recover, Christina had asked Bailey to take her home. Ray would want to be with his mom and family when he came out of it, not with her.

Bailey wondered why Christina had added the *not with me* part, but she hadn't explained. Bailey had dropped Christina off at her house, she declining Bailey's offer to stay, saying she'd rather be alone.

So Bailey had gone home to straighten the afghans on the couch and relive lying there with Adam. She'd relived making love to him again when she'd finally gone to bed, and again when she'd slept. She'd dreamed of Adam thrusting hard into her, the feeling so exact she was surprised to find herself alone when she woke up.

Today Bailey rode around the large ring on Dodie, while Grant gave commands from the ground. She was learning to hold on while Dodie reared up on cue. Grant worked them for a time, and then Bailey walked Dodie around to rest her.

Dodie's ears pricked, the mare interested in something at the rail. Bailey looked ahead and saw what had grabbed her attention, or rather—who.

Adam stood there, arms resting on the top rail, watching them. Grant raised his hand in brief greeting, and then abruptly turned away and climbed out of the ring on the far side.

"Keep walking her," Grant called back to Bailey. "She needs another couple of turns."

She didn't, but Bailey didn't argue.

Adam didn't move as Bailey rode around, as though watching her cool down a horse was the most interesting thing in the world to him. At the end of another lap, Bailey gave up and pulled Dodie to a halt next to him. Dodie stretched her head down for petting, and Adam stroked her neck.

"Hey," Adam said to Bailey.

Bailey's face went hot, and it had nothing to do with the sun. "Hey, yourself."

Adam looked better than ever, his dark hat shadowing the ruined side of his face, his stance easy. His blue eyes took her in and didn't let her go.

"I never told you what I needed help with last night," he said. "I still need it, Bailey, and I'm still gonna ask you."

No, they'd gotten ... distracted. Bailey remembered Adam's fierce anguish that had led to their bruising kisses and then lovemaking like they couldn't get enough.

"Ask me what?" Bailey gave Dodie a pat. "What could you possibly need my help with? You passed your math class years ago."

Adam didn't smile. His distress was more muted today, controlled, but it hadn't gone away.

"I need your help with this stupid-ass challenge I let Kyle talk me into." Adam's eyes darkened, whatever tortured him returning. "I'm a fucking coward, Bailey. I need you to get me over it. There's no one else I can go to about this. Only you."

# Chapter Thirteen

Adam's throat closed up after he made the declaration, not letting him say anything more.

Bailey studied him for a time from her height on the horse's back, her supple thigh at his eye level. It was all Adam could do not to stroke her instead of the horse.

Bailey slid her feet from the stirrups then swung down from Dodie, a soft puff of dust wafting upward as she landed. She slid the reins over the horse's head and folded the ends in her hand.

"What are you talking about?" she asked, her voice calm. "You're not a coward."

"You bet I am," Adam said bitterly. "I'm a total fucked-up mess." Whatever held back his words broke, and they came flowing out.

"I'm sitting on my ass, doing nothing. Mark is calling me, telling me to get back to L.A. now that I'm better, and I'm still here. I told you all the shit I've done and walked away from like it was nothing.

I'm supposed to show up Kyle at the Fall Festival, but thinking of doing any kind of stunt—hell, even getting up on Dodie and jogging around the ring—scares the shit out of me." He bunched his fist on the rail, but he didn't hit it. No sense spooking the horse. "I'm finished. It's over. I had a nice life."

"Stop it." Bailey scowled at him. She started to say more, then stopped and motioned to one of the guys who'd worked there forever as he passed the riding ring. The man nodded a greeting to Adam as he climbed through the rails, his stringy body fitting easily between the bars. Bailey handed him Dodie's reins, and without a word, the man led Dodie out of the ring and back to the barn.

Bailey faced Adam again, but remained inside the ring, the horizontal rails between them. "What's this about the Fall Festival? You took a dare from Kyle? What are you two—twelve?"

"Just about." Adam told her a truncated version of his argument with Kyle in the bar's parking lot and Kyle's throw down, eliminating the part about their contention over Bailey. "We haven't worked out the details, but it's going to be best man wins." He rested his arm on a rail, pretending not to lean his weight on it.

Bailey studied him with steady eyes, which were brown like the richest chocolate. They'd looked even better last night, half closed in pleasure.

"PTSD," she said.

Adam snapped himself back to the present. "What?"

"P—T—S—D." Bailey repeated each letter slowly. "Post-traumatic stress disorder. Or something near enough like it. You were in a bad accident, and you blame yourself for it. You almost died, but you survived, and your friend didn't. It's something you have to face."

"Trust me, I face it." Adam's jaw was tight. "I wake up every day and face it. You'd have loved Dawson, Bailey. He was the wildest, most partying guy I ever met, and at the same time, the kindest man I knew."

His eyes stung. No, this couldn't happen. Not out here, in front of Bailey, when his brothers could walk by at any time. They'd find Adam leaning on the rail, bawling like a baby, and they'd feel sorry for him.

"You have to let yourself grieve, Adam," Bailey said.

She wasn't admonishing. She just said it.

"Yeah? What the hell do you know about grief?" Adam heard the harsh words come out, but he couldn't stop them. "I lost my dad when I was ten. I had no idea how to deal with that. I couldn't cry and lock myself in the basement—I had to be the man of the family. I had responsibility. Same as now. I'm part of a business that my actions could lose, which will cost my mom her home, everything she's ever known. My brothers can handle it, but my mom shouldn't have to worry like this anymore. I can't fall apart." His scarred hand clenched the rail, whitening the skin around his knuckles. "I can't. Not now."

"I'm not telling you to fall apart," Bailey said in an even tone. "I'm telling you to let yourself grieve, to miss Dawson. He deserves that."

"Bailey, will you stop with the counseling shit? I got enough of that crap in L.A."

"No." She gave him a scowl, not moving an inch. Adam remembered that about Bailey—her shy, timid exterior hid a backbone of steel, a determination that put to shame the most hardened men he knew.

She went on. "I *do* know about grief. Catching my husband in bed with another woman kicked my ass. I grieved for a long time, missing the bastard at the same time I hated him. I didn't miss *him* — the person he revealed himself to be — I missed what we'd had. The fun, companionship. I'd relied on him, confided in him, told him things I couldn't share with anyone else. All that was taken from me in two seconds. For a long time after that, I didn't want to think or feel. I didn't have anyone to talk to, not really. I know there were plenty of people who thought it was my fault — he'd never have gone to her if I'd been keeping him happy, right?"

Bailey's fists were clenched, her eyes swimming with tears, and yet, she stood there and told Adam what had hurt her deeply, ripping the lid off what she'd kept buried.

Adam didn't like the barrier between them. He climbed smoothly up and over the railing, happy his leg didn't protest too much. He landed in front of her, boots sinking a little into the thick dirt, and she took a startled step back.

Adam followed that step. "Where does he live? Your ex? I'm going to go kick the living shit out of him."

Bailey shook herself out of her sad place and gave him a look of impatience. "Is that your answer to everything? Hitting it?"

"Pretty much. Makes me feel better, anyway."

There it was — Bailey's smile, flashing warmth through the gloom. "Well, I'm not going to tell you. You don't need *two* lawsuits."

"Hey, I've been living in California. Everyone sues everyone there, all the time. It's like a state pastime."

Bailey folded her arms. "What do you want from me, exactly? What do you want me to do?"

Adam looked her up and down, once again comforted by her nearness. It crept up on him, that comfort. Stealth comfort, Bailey-style.

"What do I want from you?" Adam let himself smile. "Hmm, how about you in a warm shower, me soaping you down, then getting on my knees, licking between your thighs …"

Bailey's face was scarlet. "*Adam!*"

"Sweetheart, you can't stand there looking all sexy and being nice to me without my brain going where it's going."

"I'm not sexy. I'm covered in horse sweat, and a little bit of horseshit."

Adam burst out laughing. He'd thought he'd never laugh again, but around Bailey, anything was possible.

"Sexy's not about what you look like," he said. "It's about what you are. And what I want from you is to be inside you. Finding out what you like. Giving that to you. But mostly just being inside you."

He liked how she gaped at him, the lush lips he wanted to kiss parted, moist. She'd never had any idea how beautiful she was, and that shithead she'd married hadn't helped. Adam wanted to punch him for every second of pain he'd caused Bailey, and then some more just for the hell of it.

He went on. "What I need you to do is get me back up on a horse. I've tried to come out here before, grab a horse, and ride off, but I can't. I pick up a saddle and start shaking. I can't figure out why, because I was on a motorcycle when I banged myself up, not a horse. But it's like I can't do anything I did with the stunt business, from riding to jumping off a wall. Was all I could do to climb the fence just now. You understand what I'm saying? You gotta help me. I don't know anyone else who can."

Bailey's blush lessened as he descended into pathetic begging, and when he finished, she regarded him in surprise. "Seems like there's a lot of people around who could help you. Your brothers. Your friends. Faith."

"I can't tell them. They'd say they understood, but they wouldn't. Not really. Carter, maybe with the crap he's gone through, might, but he'd just tell me to suck it up. And he wouldn't be wrong."

Bailey frowned. "You're still not telling me what I can do that they can't."

"Well, for one thing, you're prettier than my brothers. Come on, Bailey. I can talk to you like I can't talk to them. It's always been that way."

"Always?" She stuck her thumbs into her waistband and cocked her head. "I don't know. In high school, you never talked to me at all. Years at the same school, and you never even said hey to me in the hall. Then one day, you're smiling at me, saying, sure, you could use my help. All the sudden you think I'm the smartest girl in school, your only hope. Giving me that handsome Adam smile, enticing me into your bedroom … I'm thinking nothing's changed."

That little tilt of her head, the assessing look, was heating Adam's body. He pointed a finger at her chest. "Sweetheart, *you* were the one chasing after me in the parking lot, telling me you could help me pass my classes. My guardian angel come to life, I thought when I looked at you."

Her eyes lost their teasing light. "Save it, Adam. You charm your way into getting whatever you want, and you know it. I'll help you, all right? But you didn't have to come out here and sweet-talk me into it. You only had to ask."

"I did ask. I ran to your house last night, making a big-ass fool of myself asking. Like I'm doing now."

"No, you looked at me with your hot blue eyes and seduced the hell out of me. It's what you do." Bailey gave him a severe look. "Fine. I'll be your trainer. I'll get you riding again and into fighting shape to face Kyle. But I'm going to be a ball buster. All right? I'm not going to give you any slack for being cute."

Adam put his hand to the left side of his face, brushing his scars. "You call this cute? That's gone forever."

"Being attractive isn't about what you look like. It's what you are. Isn't that what you just said to me?"

Adam lifted his hands in surrender. "All right. Enough talk. Can we get on with this before I lose what little nerve I have left?"

Bailey's smile blossomed again. "Sure," she said. "But don't say I didn't warn you. Come on." She turned and walked toward the open barn, giving him a sexy little come-hither wiggle with her shoulder as she went.

Adam followed, because he knew by now he'd follow her anywhere, didn't matter where she wanted to go.

**

Bailey haltered the horse she thought would work best and led him out of his stall, handing the lead rope to Adam. The wide, airy, high-ceilinged barn smelled of dust, hay, and horses, the best smell in the world, in Bailey's opinion.

Adam took the rope but eyed the horse in disbelief. "Buster? You want my first day back in the saddle to be on *Buster*?"

As if in answer, Buster tried to bite him. Adam, long-experienced, evaded his teeth and pushed the horse's nose away. "See that?"

Bailey shrugged. "He doesn't bite me. He knows I'll bite him back."

Adam's gaze sharpened. "Seriously? I think I'd pay to see that."

"He and I understand each other. But he's the best horse to help you get your riding legs back. He's a shit on the ground, but once you're on, he's unspookable."

"Whatever you say," Adam conceded, but skeptically. "Let's go."

He led Buster out of the barn to the area where horses got tacked up. Adam looped the lead rope around a hitching rail, sidestepping as Buster tried to swat him with a back foot.

Adam fetched the saddle and bridle from the tack room himself while Bailey stood aside and watched. Adam's hands shook a bit as he positioned blanket and saddle a little forward on Buster's withers, then slid them back into place. Buster did his trick of sucking in a big breath while Adam fastened the cinch, but Adam knew how to poke at him until he let it out again.

Adam unhooked the rope from the halter, holding Buster by the forelock as the halter came off. In the next second, he was sliding the bridle over the horse's head, the halter hanging from his arm.

Buster had the glint in his eye he sometimes got when they tacked up—*I can bolt right now, just to prove I can.*

Adam growled as Buster started to move, and settled the bridle into place. Buster didn't want the bit—he never did—and clamped his teeth stubbornly together. Adam stuck his finger and thumb into the corners of Buster's mouth to make him open it. Buster eventually did, retaliating by letting a stream of drool flow over Adam's arm.

"I got two words for you," Adam said. "*Glue factory.*"

Buster didn't look worried. He was one of the best stunt horses they had, and he seemed to know it.

Bailey struggled to keep the grin off her face while she watched. She didn't say so, but Buster's antics had made Adam forget to be afraid. He was growling and swearing instead, the haunted look for now erased from his eyes.

It came back, though, when Adam handed Bailey the empty halter and led Buster out to an open area to mount.

Adam stilled next to Buster—who whacked Adam with his tail—holding the reins as his limbs stiffened.

"I don't know, Bailey," he said. "At least I got this far."

"Nope." Bailey folded her arms. "We're done when I say we're done."

Adam gave her his eye-crinkling smile. "You know, you're sexy when you're bossy."

"Nice try. Put the reins over his head, and get on that horse. I'll give you a leg-up if you need it."

"I haven't needed a leg-up since I was three. And then only because I was really short." Adam's words were light and quick, hiding the tremor in his voice.

He took his time lifting the reins over Buster's head to rest them on his neck. Buster had to make a show of trying to bite again, but less enthusiastically this time.

Adam put his left hand still holding the reins on the front of the saddle, made to lift his foot to the stirrup, then suddenly bowed his head and rested his forehead on the seat.

"Bailey," he said, his voice barely audible. "Damn it. I'm having a hard time breathing here."

# Chapter Fourteen

Bailey went quickly to him, speaking in a soft voice, her heart beating hard. "You're all right. You're home, Adam. You're with me."

She stood right behind him, his back to her chest. Adam raised his head, but he stood still, and she felt his chest expand as he took a long breath.

"I know," he said. "It's just ..." He took another deep breath. "I don't know how I'm going to get up there."

"Here." Bailey caught Adam's jeans' leg at his left ankle and raised his foot to the stirrup. Adam gave her a startled glance, but before he could argue, she put her hands on his backside and pushed. "Up you go."

His ass was fine, and she had a hard time taking her hands off it. Adam swung his right leg over, settled into the saddle, and glared down at her.

"That's *not* how you give a leg-up," he said.

Bailey smiled. "It's how I do it—with you."

"Wipe that grin off your face. If you give anyone else a boost like that, I'll kill him."

"Nope. Only you. Now walk him to the covered ring."

Adam gave her an irritated look but turned Buster and headed him for the long, covered ring where the brothers trained for their acts. The huge roof let them ride even in the rain and also protected them from the brutal sun in the summer.

Buster walked slowly, as though wanting Bailey, on foot, to keep up. Adam sat well, despite his injury, his body knowing how to ride. He was fine physically, but the bleak light in his eyes worried her.

They reached the ring and Bailey opened the gate. Adam turned Buster in, looking up at the roof as though he'd never seen it before. Buster moved to the rail and started around, familiar with the routine.

Bailey shut the gate, moved to the middle of the fence, and climbed up to sit on the top rail. "A couple times around to warm up," Bailey called. "He hasn't been off his butt all morning."

Adam lifted his hand to show he'd heard, and kept Buster going at his quick walk.

Watching Adam in the saddle was a treat. He'd been riding his whole life, and it showed in the way he moved with the horse, relaxed and easy but upright and alert. His jeans stretched over hard legs and a tight backside; his shirt molded to a well-honed torso. His black hat, which he kept in place even under the arena roof, only enhanced the picture of the long, tall, *hot* Texan.

"Pick him up," Bailey said after Adam and Buster had gone around a second time. She almost forgot to give the order in the pleasure of watching Adam's body at work.

Buster moved into a jog on his next step. If Adam had signaled him, it had been so subtle Bailey missed it, which was as it should be. Either that or Buster heard her—he recognized a number of voice commands.

Rider and horse began moving in what looked like a lazy pace, but Bailey knew they were going well. "Bring him up the middle," she said after they'd gone around a few times more. "We'll put him through some easy moves, to get you used to it again. All right?"

Adam didn't answer. He rode Buster straight up the middle of the ring the long way, then guided him to circle right or left at Bailey's order. She worked them at a trot then a lope, Buster changing his lead as he switched direction at Adam's command.

Bailey remembered sitting in the stands at the Fall Festival and at rodeos, watching Adam ride and falling in love with him. He'd been energetic and still at the same time, moving lithely with his horse, his quiet expertise filling Bailey's fantasies.

Nothing had changed. Man and horse moved together in the ring, gliding, turning. Adam sat quietly, one hand loose on his thigh, while he expertly reined the horse and guided him with his body.

Bailey wasn't falling in love with him again, she'd already fallen. Hard—as though she'd been tossed from a horse and lay on the ground, winded and dirty.

Adam was going fine now, riding Buster in figure eights and more complicated patterns, again at the jog, then slow lope, then picking up speed at an extended canter. Bailey would never have believed that Adam had lost his nerve if he hadn't told her, in a voice so full of despair she knew he wasn't faking it.

He'd come to her to help him regain his confidence. Once he had it back, he'd be packing his bags and running off again to his movie life.

And why wouldn't he? Adam's talents were in high demand, he made a lot of money, and he had a ton of friends out in California, plus a mentor who looked out for him. His lawyers would deal with the lawsuit, and Adam would be on top of his game again. Out of Bailey's life and back to his own.

She was sitting here helping him leave her. Bailey could have refused, but that meant letting Adam decide to hide for the rest of his life and not deal with his pain. No, wait, he wouldn't hide—he'd find someone else to help him and never forgive Bailey for letting him dangle.

Either way, Bailey lost.

She thought of the raw pain she'd seen in Adam's eyes when he'd come to her last night. *For God's sake, you've got to help me.*

Bailey couldn't turn her back on him, and she knew it.

"Looking good," she called. "Want to take him out on the trail? I'll get a horse and come with you."

Adam turned Buster and rode him straight at Bailey. When he halted alongside her, she saw that his face was wan and drawn, his eyes fixed, sweat beading on his skin.

"No," he said, voice tight. "I'm barely doing this. I want to throw up."

Bailey looked at him in surprise. "But you looked great out there."

"I know how to ride. I mean, my body does. It took over. My brain is months behind. If I do anything but ride around in pretty circles, I'll lose it. No way am I going to beat Kyle at anything by the Fall Festival. I'm screwed."

Bailey had only seen Adam afraid once in his life, and that had been when he'd gotten the news he might not graduate. Then it had not been so much fear but shame and uncertainty. This was rock-solid terror.

"Bring Buster closer," she said abruptly.

"What?"

"I'm coming up behind you."

Adam stared at her a moment, then he slowly moved Buster until his rump was an inch from the rail. Bailey used Adam's shoulder to steady herself as she slid over Buster's back and settled onto the blanket behind the saddle's high cantle.

Buster never flinched, holding still until Bailey found her balance and wrapped her arms around Adam's middle.

"Now ride."

Adam didn't move. "What the hell are you doing?"

"Buster is used to having two on him. Come on. We have a lot of work to do."

**

Adam's world changed as soon as Bailey's arms closed around him. He'd been riding on automatic, fixed in his watery dread, willing himself not to go into a panic attack. The one last night while he'd faced Kyle had been bad, and he didn't want to go through that again anytime soon.

Once Bailey was balancing behind him, her warmth enveloping him, his focus shifted to her. Nothing else was important.

"To*day*, Adam," came her stern voice at his back.

He wasn't wrong about her being sexy when she was bossy. Adam's jaw unclenched enough to allow him a faint chuckle.

"Yes, *ma'am*," he said, then nudged Buster forward.

One of the stable hands let them out of the gate. They rode across the open space between rings and barn, toward another gate that led to open land and riding trails.

Apparently, no one else at the ranch had anything better to do than watch Adam and Bailey ride out. The hired hands leaned on rakes and brooms or paused on their way into and out of the barn. Grant, Tyler, and Carter, along with a couple guys they were training, stopped their horses and turned to watch.

All were silent as Bailey and Adam walked slowly past on Buster and made for the far gate. Bailey waved, but Adam pretended to utterly ignore them.

"Someday my brothers will mind their own business," Adam said after he'd leaned down and unlatched the gate for them, taken Buster through, and closed it up again. "It'll be really cold that day in hell too. Pigs will be flying around all over the place …"

"They're worried about you."

Bailey's sweet voice, so close, relaxed him another notch. "They're nosy," Adam growled. "It'll be all over town by tonight that you were on a horse with me, hugging me tight."

"Oh, well, so what if it is?"

Adam let out another chuckle. He really didn't mind if the whole town knew that Adam and Bailey were together. Kyle could eat shit.

Bailey became all business again. "Take the north trail. Once we get up the hill, put him into a trot."

Adam stiffened. Buster felt his tension and swished his tail. "I don't want you falling off," Adam said.

"I know how to fall," Bailey said. "So do you. It's the first thing we learn. We'll be doing that later. We also know how *not* to fall."

She sounded so logical, as though Adam was in control of everything he did.

But the sun was warm, Bailey behind him was warmer, and it was a fine Texas late-September day. If he didn't think too much, he could ride, guiding Buster with his weight, giving him the slightest touch with reins and legs. Bailey was a glorious distraction, with her arms firmly around Adam's waist, he steadying her at the same time she steadied him.

They made it to the top of the hill, and Buster moved into a jog with the barest nudge from Adam.

Adam could do this, he thought. He'd been riding since he could walk, and stunt riding for years. The Campbell boys were fearless—at least, that's what everyone said.

Buster jogged along, liking to be out. Bailey had been right to put Adam on him—in spite of his bad manners, Buster was solid and knew his job.

They rode down the other side of the low hill, the gentle green just fading from its grass. The rise hid the house, barns, and rings behind them. No one would be able to watch them out here unless they deliberately followed, which was likely why Bailey had chosen this trail. Adam wouldn't put it past his brothers to find some excuse to be out here, though, so he urged Buster to go a little faster.

"Great," Bailey said brightly behind him. "Take him into a lope, and we'll practice some falls."

*Shit.* Adam's vision began to cloud, and the roar of the accident started to blot out all other sound.

"Not yet," he managed to say. "Let me get used to this first."

"Your whole business is falling," Bailey said in a reasonable tone. "Getting your nerve for it back is the first thing you need to work on."

"Bailey ..." The flames were coming for him again.

Bailey's arms tightened around his waist. "It's all right, Adam. I'll catch you."

Oh, right. Adam would fall on her and squash her. What the hell was she talking about?

*She sure looks good,* Dawson's drawl came to him over the noise in his head.

Adam had once shown Dawson a photo of Bailey that his mom had sent him. The picture had dated from after Bailey had graduated from college and begun her first job in Austin. She'd started pulling her hair back from her gorgeous face by that time, and in the picture, wore a dress that, while modest, didn't completely hide her curves.

Dawson had said, *You left that behind? Are you crazy?*

Yes, Adam had been crazy. Craving a fast-paced existence, money for his family, approval. He'd been seduced by the movie business and brushed aside his home life. And Bailey.

*She's with you now,* Dawson's voice went on, and Adam wondered what his messed-up brain was doing to him this time. *Keep her there.*

Messed-up brain or not, whether Dawson was reaching out to him or not, the man was right.

"We can fall tomorrow," Adam said over his shoulder. "Let's just enjoy the ride."

"Nope. You're going to move your lazy ass." Bailey wasn't taking any shit today. "Ride him over to where we practice."

Grant, Tyler, and Carter had raked out a flat area, still on Campbell land, and hauled out extra dirt and shavings to make a landing place for practice falls. They rehearsed more difficult stunts there, the ones that needed a lot of room.

"We'll do something easy at first," Bailey said. "Get some momentum, and then take a dive."

Adam's throat closed up, his mouth drying. But he sucked in a breath and told his brain to calm down. He could do this.

He approached the beginning of the run and put Buster into a lope. Buster knew the drill. He moved on, picking up speed into a faster canter, which scooped Bailey tight against Adam. *Good horse.*

"Like this," Bailey called, and then her warmth was gone, and there was empty space where she'd been.

Adam swung back to see Bailey heading for the ground, tucking in her arms, letting her shoulder take the fall, rolling with it. A good landing, but

Adam wheeled Buster around in alarm, vaulting out of the saddle before he was aware of what he was doing.

He landed on his feet, but his busted-up leg bent. He went down into a roll, automatically coming out of it and ending up on his feet again.

He ran to Bailey, reached down, and pulled her up. "What the fuck?" he demanded.

Bailey broke his hold to brush herself off. She had dirt on her cheek, dried grass in her hair.

Adam pulled at the bits of grass, distracted by her softness. "You all right?" he asked.

Bailey regarded him in surprise. "I'm fine. Your brothers trained me." She grinned. "I meant to do that."

"I know." Adam tightened his grip. "But seeing you fall … I don't like it."

Bailey's bright smile vanished. "We've had this discussion before. I love to ride. I love the stunts. I had a great time on that shoot with Grant while you were recovering. When I'm riding, I feel alive. It's the only thing that knocked me awake after my awful divorce, and I'm not letting you take it away from me. Understand?"

# Chapter Fifteen

Adam went still as Bailey's voice rose with her agitation. If he wasn't comfortable with himself when he was in danger of crying, he was even worse when women started in, Bailey in particular.

Her smiles were gone, her face was flushed, her eyes bright. This was important to her—desperately important. Adam got that, but all he wanted to do was protect her. He didn't care about anything else right now, not even Buster flipping his tail as he ran for the hills.

"I'm not trying to take it away from you," Adam said, impatient. "I'm trying to keep you safe."

Bailey planted her hands on her hips, furious at him—again. "Well, you can't. *Life* isn't safe. It's always waiting to whack us in the ass when we least expect it. People get hurt. Friends and family die. We can't stop it. We have to grab on to what we have, and love the people we love as hard as we can while we still have them. 'Cause you never know what shit will happen."

Bailey's eyes shone with tears. "Hey." Adam rested his hands on her shoulders. "I'm not trying to take anything from you. But thinking of you being hurt—that kind of kills me inside."

The tears overflowed. "Stop it. Stop pretending you want to take care of me. I take care of myself just fine."

"I'm not pretending." Adam stepped back, unable to keep still in his rising anger. "You want to know what the worst thing is for a guy? To see a woman we care about hurting. It makes us want to hit something. Makes it worse when we can't do anything about it."

Bailey wiped her eyes with the back of her hand. "You're very macho."

"It's the truth. That's why we walk away sometimes and don't say anything. We're trying to figure out how to make it better. We don't always know. And that's hard."

Bailey swiped away the last of her tears. "I told you I'd help you, and I will. But don't take something from me that makes me want to get up in the morning. I spent a lot of mornings wondering why I should bother."

"You're not making me like that bastard you married any better. You sure you won't tell me where he lives? He still in Austin? I'm thinking about making the drive. Maybe taking Carter with me."

Bailey gave him a weak grin. "Much as I'd like to see that ... I don't want you arrested for assault on top of everything else."

"I have good lawyers and know a lot of cops." Adam moved closer to her. "I guess we've both been beaten up. We're both hurting—maybe we should have stayed home and left the world alone." He took her dirty hand between his. "It's you and me now, Bailey. How about we help each other?"

She flushed a brighter red, her agitated look gone. Adam hoped she'd step against him, agreeing, maybe sealing the bargain with a kiss, but instead, she did a brief eye-roll.

"You're back to being a sweet-talker, aren't you?" She gave him an exasperated look, then turned to scan the hills. "Don't you think we should catch Buster? He'll be halfway to the highway by now."

**

Buster had stopped on the next rise, his head down, nibbling grass around his bit. He paid no attention to Adam, no matter how much Adam whistled and called.

When Bailey cupped her hands around her mouth and shouted his name, Buster lifted his head and came trotting back. Reluctantly, but he came.

Adam shot Bailey a dark look as she caught the reins, which by some miracle had stayed around Buster's neck and hadn't broken. "Did you do witchcraft on him or something?"

"No." Bailey patted Buster. "He likes women, is all."

"Him and me both. All right, Bailey." Adam opened his hands and gave her his best charming look. "I'm done pissing you off for the day. Let's ride."

Bailey stayed on the ground, and Adam, who seemed a little more relaxed, rode up and down the practice area, getting comfortable in the saddle once more.

She got lost watching him again, Adam's riding skills even more obvious out in the open. His hat kept his face shaded, only the glitter of his eyes flashing as he looked around.

He made a timeless picture. If a hundred years fell away, Adam wouldn't look out of place at all, riding easily along the rolling hills, a son of Texas under endless sky.

Bailey watched until she convinced herself she should do something more than admire him. She cleared her throat of dust.

"Ready?" she called out.

Adam turned Buster and loped back. "Depends. What are you going to make me do?"

"How about a dead-man ride?"

She clapped her mouth shut over the words as soon as she said them. Though it was the Campbells' term for the move, she worried it would trigger Adam's anger or grief. Adam only gave her a nod. "Sure. Cue me."

He took off his hat, dropped it to her as he went by, then rode Buster down to the end of the run. Bailey watched him halt the horse, square his shoulders, and then put Buster into a gallop.

As he passed, Bailey yelled, "Bang!"

Buster, knowing the drill, came off his front legs a few inches, then plunged back down again, running on. Adam faked taking a bullet, letting his arms fly open, then his body went limp.

They had several ways they played dead in the saddle. Slumped forward, falling back flat, or dangling off one side. Adam chose to go backward over the cantle, his feet still in the stirrups, his arms flopping as though the hero of the show had potted him good. Adam did it so well that Bailey bit her lip. Too realistic. No wonder stunt coordinators wanted him.

Buster kept going until the end of the run, then he slowed to a walk. He'd done his part; the take was over.

Adam heaved himself up, regained his seat, and rode back to Bailey. "That was stiff," he said. "I'm out of practice."

"Not the point." Bailey held his hat in front of her, but he didn't reach for it. "How did that feel?"

"*Stiff*," Adam repeated. "But I know what you're asking. Not bad. I'm kind of running on automatic pilot."

"That's good." Bailey gave him an encouraging smile. "It means you're relaxing. Not getting in your own way."

He frowned. "If this is supposed to be therapy, it's not working."

"Don't be a shit. This is me helping you get ready to whup Kyle's ass at the Fall Festival."

Adam's eyes narrowed. "Why do you want me to so bad? I thought you liked Kyle."

She flushed. "I do, but he had no business challenging you. I didn't think picking on an injured man was his style."

Something flickered in Adam's eyes, but he only shrugged. "We've always torn it up. Come on, I won't win doing simple falls or taking fake shots. Everyone in town will expect to see me up to what I used to do. I need to get to work."

He sounded better, looked better. The lines around Adam's eyes were tight, but his face was set with determination.

Bailey sent him off again. He practiced more dead-man rides, falling forward on the horse, arms and legs dangling, then hanging on to the saddle while half falling off the side as Buster kept running. Buster was best for this, because he didn't mind his rider's weight shifting around. He compensated and did what he loved best—run.

Adam agreed to try some falls after a while. Easy ones at first, dives and rolls, which had him quickly back on his feet. The dirt and shavings were at least a foot and a half thick—Adam told her it provided more padding from riding falls than he got on many movie shoots.

Finally, he let himself go over backwards, tumbling from Buster's rump to land in a heap, again so realistically that Bailey couldn't prevent herself running over to him.

Adam rolled to a sitting position, looking fine as she bent over him.

"It's hot," was all he said, taking his hat from her. "Let's take a break."

Afternoon had come, and with it heat. September might be fall in other places in the country, but here temperatures still climbed into the nineties, sometimes breaking a hundred.

Buster would need to rest as well. He was always game to work, but ruining him in the heat was not what Bailey had in mind.

"We missed lunch," Bailey said, checking the time. "Maybe your mom kept something for us."

"You hungry?" Adam asked, sounding surprised.

"Not really. But I thought you wanted to go back to the house."

"No, I said I wanted to take a break. Call Buster. We'll need him."

Bailey, mystified, shouted for Buster, who returned, lolling along, unconcerned. Adam mounted without assistance, then held his hand down for Bailey to join him.

Before she could scramble onto the back of the saddle, Adam grabbed her and sat her down cross-ways in front of him. He started Buster off at a slow jog, flashing Bailey a brief grin.

His eyes were dark blue under the hat's shading brim, the shadow obscuring the ruined part of his face. He was handsome Adam again, sweeping Bailey off her feet — this time literally.

Adam rode away from the training area, up another hill, and down into a valley where a branch of the river cut in. The inlet was deep, surrounded by trees, a good place for swimming or lazing around in rowboats.

No boaters were there today. Adam took Buster at a walk along the path that led to the inlet's shore, a wide, flat spot that backed onto a narrow dirt road. The rutted road was the only access to the place for vehicles; it was much easier to approach down trails on horseback.

Adam lowered Bailey from the saddle, then swung off, dropped the reins, loosened the cinch, and dragged the saddle down. He pulled off the bridle as well. Buster trotted about two feet before his head was down, the horse nibbling grass. Now that he was free to run, he wouldn't — he was like that.

Adam hung his hat on the nearest tree branch and peeled off his shirt.

"What are you ..." Bailey trailed off as his hard torso came into view, slick with sweat and touched by sunshine.

Adam put his hand to his belt buckle. "Going for a swim. What do you think I'm doing?"

His belt came off, then his boots.

"*Adam.*"

The word was strangled as Adam unzipped his jeans and slid them down and off with his underwear.

Adam naked in the sunlight was the most beautiful thing she'd ever seen. Didn't matter that his body was scarred and still healing, it was hard, tight, strong. Nothing wrong with him.

He'd stripped down last night, but they'd been in a rush, and Bailey hadn't had the chance to appreciate him fully. Now she looked, taking her time.

Wide shoulders topped hard, honed pectorals, Adam's chest dusted with dark, curling hair, burnished now by sunshine. His waist was flat, navel a shadow, and another line of hair pointed enticingly downward. His legs were strong, balancing the weight of him perfectly.

What the glory trail pointed to grabbed Bailey's attention and wouldn't let go. He was half erect under her scrutiny, making her remember him fully hard last night. She imagined the feel of his cock in her hand as she glided her fingers along it, the heavy tip bumping her palm. She could be kneeling before him, sun warm on her back, as she let him slip into her mouth ...

She made a noise in her throat and hugged her arms over herself, shivering despite the heat.

Adam gave her his slow smile, the one that said he knew she wanted him. He was arrogant, full of himself, and broken, all at the same time.

She pointed a shaking finger at the river. "Water's over there."

"I know that." Adam retrieved his hat, completing the knee-weakening portrait by setting it on his head. "I'm waiting for you to join me."

Bailey couldn't have taken her eyes off him if she'd tried. "There might be snakes." Of course there would be. The whole state was crawling with them.

Adam shrugged. "I'll scare them away. Come on."

He delivered the command in his slow drawl, the old Adam returning. He gave her a final look, then walked the few feet across the dried grass to the water.

The back of him was as good as the front. He strode, head up, hat firmly on, the sun kissing down his back to the firm muscle of his ass.

*I am the luckiest girl in the world, just seeing that.*

"Come on, Bailey," he called. "You chicken?" He made clucking noises as he turned around and sank into the water, pushing off to swim on his back.

He wanted her to strip off all her clothes and run into the water with him. She'd be crazy to. Or maybe she'd be crazy not to.

Bailey gave the surrounding area a quick glance, making sure they were truly alone, then she fumbled off her clothes as rapidly as she could. She hung them on the limb next to Adam's and started for the water.

Adam stood up, water lapping his hips, watching her come. He was looking over Bailey as hard as she'd looked over him, and she hoped he liked what he saw.

Cool water closed over her then, making her gasp. Adam's smile widened, and he swam lazily to her.

"Hey," he said, his voice low. Water beaded on his lashes, his blue eyes dark. "Ain't you pretty?"

Bailey went hot, never mind the coldness of the water and mud sucking at her toes. She didn't notice anything but Adam's warm gaze, and his hands coming up to rest on her shoulders.

"Remember when I said what I mostly wanted was to be inside you?" Adam waited until Bailey gave him a frozen nod. "I figure, if I can stay inside you as much as I can, then the rest of the shit in this world won't matter."

Bailey wet her lips, which shook. "You can't hide from life by having sex all the time."

"Why the hell not? Sex is life, Bailey. It's the most basic part of life. Without it, there *is* no life."

"I suppose you've got a point."

"You bet I do." He paused. "You never had kids."

"What?" Bailey blinked at the incongruity. "No, no I didn't. We said we'd wait."

No, *Lawrence* had said they'd wait. Until they had more money, a bigger house, higher positions in the company, whatever his excuse had been each time. Bailey realized now that kids would have taken his attention from what he wanted — wealth, success, his own pleasure.

"Bet you'd make a great mom," Adam said.

Bailey's heart filled with longing. "I never really thought about it." *Liar.*

"When we do have kids, you can tell them." Adam carefully removed his hat, floated up out of the water, and snagged it on an overhanging branch. "You can tell them what we did together in the swimming hole." He grinned. "When they're old enough. We can embarrass them."

Did he mean having kids with her? she wondered, her heart pounding. Or was he talking about children who'd come along at some point in each of their lives?

Bailey stopped thinking when Adam slid his arms around her, pulling his wet body into hers, and slanted a warm kiss across her mouth.

**

Bailey was like sunshine in his arms. Adam tasted heat as he brought her closer still. The water let them come face-to-face without impediment, all the better for Adam to hold her, kiss her.

Nothing he'd seen in his life had been more beautiful than Bailey running bare into the water. Her breasts had moved with her stride, sunlight pouring down on her, heaven picking her out in a beam of light.

She might be an angel sent to guide him, but she was also a flesh-and-blood woman. Adam slid his hands down her back as he kissed her, fingers on her soft buttocks, lifting her to wrap her legs around him.

The cold water hadn't deflated his cock at all, and Bailey against it had him hard and ready. Her breasts crushed into his chest, the warm scent of her surrounding him as she kissed him back.

She was seriously kissing him, nibbling his lips, licking them, opening his mouth with her tongue.

She was discovering what she liked, what he liked, and Adam was fine with letting her.

He kissed her thoroughly in return, teasing behind her lips, rocking his head back as she rose up to take more.

Bailey made a sexy sound in her throat as Adam further spread her legs, pushing himself inside her without much effort.

She stopped as he thrust into her, her eyes widening for a brief moment before they took on that languid look Bailey got when she felt deepest pleasure.

Adam was a long way inside her, farther than last night, when he'd been rushed and needy. That had been good, but much too quick. Touching her last night had made him come fast, his wanting for her bottled up far too long.

Now they had a little time. He lowered her all the way onto him, his body flushing as he felt the goodness of her. She was hot and tight, Bailey holding him without shame.

She loved sex. She'd loved it back in the day, when Adam had taught it to her. Bailey hadn't been embarrassed, or grown angry at him afterward, refusing to speak to him. Nor had she broken down, full of regret for giving him her virginity. She'd kissed him, loved him, and asked to do it again.

Adam had been proud of himself for making her feel that way, but he now had enough experience to know that Bailey's unapologetic enthusiasm was rare. She could be a firecracker in bed, sweet and modest out of it, and true to herself the whole time.

Adam rocked back, bracing his feet on the riverbed as he thrust into her the best he could. The water helped, letting him bring her down to him, pleasure burning with every stroke.

He cupped Bailey's face, loving to look at her. "You are so beautiful."

Bailey hummed in her throat. "Adam," she whispered. Then she was kissing him again, too far gone for words.

She was even more beautiful when she came. Bailey clung to him, taking her pleasure, her head loose, her lips parted with her incoherent sounds. She loved every second of her climax, which pressed her tighter on Adam, squeezing him, moving her body to thrust with him.

She rode him hard, every stroke sending Adam into a wild place. He stood there and took it. A beautiful woman in his arms, wanting him, knowing how to pleasure him as she pleasured herself, was the most astonishingly erotic thing he'd ever experienced.

Adam tried to hold himself back, to let her find the peak of her coming and enjoy the white-hot fire she blazed through him. But his body wouldn't cooperate. It wanted to release, to take him into a place of mindless joy, where nothing could touch him.

A shout tore out of him at the same time his seed did, finding a home in Bailey. She held him close, her kisses untamed, taking what Adam gave and giving it hard back.

They came together, Bailey a crazed thing, Adam growing stiller and stiller as intense pleasure took him.

Once again, he and Bailey were one for a single hot, moment. Then they were two people, holding on to each other, kissing, loving, while cool water flowed around them under the scorching Texas sun.

**

"Bye, you two!"

A shrill voice rang out from the shore. Bailey jerked her head up, rising out of the warm haze she'd descended into after she and Adam had calmed.

Adam had held her easily after they'd finished, Bailey's head on his shoulder, feeling the thrum of his heartbeat. Adam bent to kiss her from time to time, but mostly they stood, wrapped in each other, enjoying the stillness and silence.

Now Bailey looked around in alarm. Buster was halfway up the hill, his bridle restored, a little girl perched on his bare back.

Faith grinned and waved at Adam and Bailey as they stared at her, Adam making sure Bailey's body stayed hidden by his and the water. Laughing, Faith turned Buster and expertly trotted him on up the hill, leaving them behind.

"Faith!" Bailey called. She struggled out of Adam's arms, shivering as her feet touched the rocky, muddy bottom.

Adam hauled Bailey back before she could plunge out of the water in all her nakedness. A stream of giggles came back to them, but Faith was gone.

"You know, sometimes I think she's the sweetest little girl alive," Adam said as they watched her disappear. "And then she proves she's Carter's daughter."

"Doesn't matter." Bailey rubbed her arms, cold without Adam against her. "The walk will do us good. Give us a chance to dry off." She spoke with more conviction than she felt. It was more than a mile back to the house, with a lot of hill climbing thrown in.

Adam leapt to grab his hat from the branch with a dripping hand. He started for the shore, pausing to give Bailey's backside a caress. Bailey watched Adam's fine rear view emerge from the river, a beautiful man nude in the sunshine.

"Damn it," Adam growled as he shrugged on his shirt. "Now I have to carry that effing saddle all the way back up the hill."

Bailey made herself climb out of the water. "We'll carry it between us. A burden shared is a burden halved, they say."

Adam reached a scarred hand down to help her, his long-sleeved shirt dangling, unbuttoned. He pulled her the rest of the way from the water and caught her around the waist.

"Stop being so damn cute," he said, then kissed her hard on the lips.

Bailey softened to him, arms going around him, loving the feel of his sunbaked clothes on her damp skin.

He deepened the kiss, a strong man loving his lady, and then he straightened up, gave her another pat on the backside, and moved off to dress and retrieve the saddle.

**\*\***

Adam was late to dinner that night. By the time he and Bailey made it up the hill and put away the saddle, the other brothers had started shutting down for the evening. The horses were being fed, including Buster, who bared his teeth at Adam when Adam went to check on him. Ungrateful shit.

When they'd reached the ranch, Bailey had hurried immediately to her truck and driven off. Grant had come out of the barn to watch the dust rise in her wake.

"Where's she going in such a hurry?"

Adam shrugged, pretending that today had been just a normal day. That he hadn't made a breakthrough, and then had sex with the most beautiful woman on the planet—outside, in water.

"Bailey had things to do," Adam said. "I'm starving." Without another word, he strode to the house, feeling Grant's puzzled stare on his back.

At the table, the family talked animatedly as usual. Ross had come for dinner, being off this evening.

Adam didn't pay much attention to them, letting their conversations flow over him. Something important had happened to him today—Bailey had planted inside him the idea that he might someday forgive himself. He turned the thought over in his mind, wondering what to do with it.

"Ray Malory will be just fine," Olivia said from the other end of the table, her silver bracelets, which she wore whenever she wasn't riding, clinking softly. "Christina told me. He's home now, with his mother looking after him. I guess that's going around." She winked at Adam.

"Good," Grant said, a little too loudly. Under his breath as he lifted his drink, he said, "Now I can kill him."

"I have some news," Faith said, her voice cutting through the conversations. All eyes turned to her, expecting her to announce some achievement at school. Though the teachers in Riverbend had thrown up their hands in despair at Faith's father and most of her uncles, the little girl got high grades and was unreservedly adored by many of those same teachers.

"What's that, baby?" Carter asked her. His love for Faith showed in everything he did. The only softness the man had in him was reserved for his daughter.

Faith shot a wicked look to the head of the table. "I saw Adam. And Bailey. At the river." Her face screwed up into a big smile. *"Skinny-dipping!"*

# Chapter Sixteen

There was dead silence a moment, then the dining room erupted in noise. "Woo-ooo!" Tyler yelled. "I *knew* it!"

Grant had taken a drink of iced tea, and now he snorted and coughed, trying to swallow and laugh at the same time.

"Good thing *I* didn't see you doing that," Ross said, his face creased with laughter. "I'd have had to arrest you. My brother and his girl, in the lock-up for public indecency. I might have let you put your clothes back on before I hauled you in. *Might.*"

Grant cleared his airways and laughed for real. "No wonder Bailey hightailed it out of here." He gave Faith a one-armed hug and a kiss on top of her head. "You are the sweetest thing, baby."

The only ones not laughing out loud were Carter and Olivia. Adam's mom watched him speculatively, as though she waited for something. Carter wore a quiet smile and looked at Adam as though understanding him for the first time.

Adam's face burned, and he reached for a glass of cold water. But somehow, he didn't mind their laughter as much as he thought he would.

*My brother and his girl,* Ross had said.

They weren't surprised at all. Nor were they condemning. As though it had been inevitable that Adam and Bailey would find their way together.

Faith didn't have any doubt. She started to sing. *"Adam and Bailey, sittin' in a tree."* Tyler and Grant joined in, their deep voices blending with her small one. *"K-i-s-s-i-n-g."*

Adam picked up his fork and went back to eating, letting them laugh at him. The cold inside him was easing off under their smiles. It felt good.

**

The story of Bailey and Adam in the river was all over town by the next day. Bailey had one calm evening of freedom from it, but when she went to pick up a few groceries the next morning, knowing smiles from every customer in the store turned in her direction.

The woman who owned the little corner grocery grinned across the counter at Bailey. "Adam's such a handsome boy, isn't he?" she said as she rang up and bagged Bailey's purchases. "Any announcements we should know about?"

Bailey flushed and grabbed the filled bag. "No. Um ... no. It's not ... not what you think."

"Of course not, dear." She looked wise. "Don't forget your card."

Bailey swung back, snatched her bank card from the woman's hand, and fled. Delighted laughter followed her.

Not everyone was laughing, Bailey discovered at the gas station, where she'd stopped to put air in her tires. A tall, willowy blond woman, who'd been one of Adam's girlfriends in high school, approached as Bailey straightened up from the machine, wiping black smears off her hands.

"You're not Adam's type," the woman announced, looking Bailey up and down. Bailey remembered her well—Donna didn't live in Riverbend anymore but in a big house with her oilman husband west of here. She'd been homecoming queen that last fall in high school, with Adam, of course, as her king.

"Adam's different now," Bailey said. "I've known him a long time."

Donna's lifted brows said she was skeptical. "He's not cut out to be a small-town boy. I knew that when we were going together. He wanted out of here, while I was happy to settle down near home. I bet he hasn't changed *that* much."

Bailey had no idea. Adam was a charmer, and even without Kyle's warning, she'd always known he didn't stick with one woman for long. Donna was living proof—she and Adam had been broken up by that Christmas.

Donna gave Bailey another once-over. "I thought you got married. Right? After you went off to Austin?"

"I did." Bailey lifted her chin. No reason to hide. "Divorced last year."

"Oh, well." Donna looked superior in her secure marriage to a rich man twice her age. "It doesn't always work out."

"No, it doesn't," Bailey agreed. Nothing else to say, really. Except *bitch*.

"Don't break your heart on Adam," Donna advised, adjusting her designer silk cardigan as she turned back to her Mercedes convertible. "He's not worth it. Trust me."

*Bitch, bitch, bitch.*

If Donna thought Adam not worth it, she didn't know him. Had never known him. Lucky for Adam.

Donna drove languidly away, leaving Bailey to fume. She made herself feel better by buying another pie from Mrs. Ward—who also hinted that she was waiting for a happy announcement from Bailey about Adam.

That night, Bailey decided to go to the bar with Christina when she went in to work, to make herself face people and talk to them. She refused to hide in her house just because the whole damn town knew she'd had sex with Adam.

Well, they only *really* knew she'd gone swimming naked with him, but they'd extrapolated. Besides, Adam might come in tonight, and she needed to talk to him.

Kyle Malory entered, followed by his big friend Jack. Kyle saw Bailey, hesitated, but stopped next to the barstool where she sat and ordered a beer from Christina.

"Hey, Kyle," Bailey said, trying to sound friendly. "How's Ray?"

Kyle shrugged, not looking at her. "He's fine," he said, also pretending to be friendly. "Whining and moaning, but fine. Doc says he's out of danger and just needs to heal a little."

"I've been fixing him chicken soup," Christina said brightly as she drew a beer from the tap for Kyle. "Nature's perfect cure."

Her smile was too brittle. Christina had been stiff, touchy, and unhappy since the accident. Bailey had seen that, but she had the feeling that right now was not a good time to push her sister. Christina would tell her what was up when she was ready.

Kyle didn't appear to notice. He took his beer and turned to Bailey as Christina moved to serve Jack.

"I heard about you and Adam," he said. "I couldn't *not* hear about it. At least twenty people stopped me this morning and told me. But don't worry. I know when to step out of the way." Kyle paused. "Tell me the truth, though—were you with him when you were going out with me?"

"No." Bailey frowned at him. "I told you, I'd never do that." Why was he so quick to believe she'd cheat on him, when she'd been cheated on herself? Adam had been worried about it too at first. They all should realize she'd be the last person do such a thing.

*Fear*, she decided. *We're all so afraid of betrayal.*

"Okay." Kyle gave her a conceding look. "But when he runs back to L.A. and his movie chicks ..." He tailed off, as though reconsidering what he'd been about to say. His grin broke through. "Give me a call."

"Sure, Kyle."

Kyle turned away ... to find Adam standing directly behind him.

\*\*

"Adam," Kyle said, giving him a faint nod.

Kyle's voice was neutral, not threatening, but his eyes told a different story. He was furious at Adam, but Adam couldn't be paid to care.

"Heard your brother was on the mend," Adam said, also playing it cool. "That's good."

"Yeah, he'll be up in no time."

"Accidents are tough," Adam said. "Give him my best."

"Sure." Kyle looked him up and down, then a spark lit his eyes. "You gonna be ready to eat dirt?"

Adam waited for the clamor of the wreck, the hot flames of the fire, to fill his head, as Kyle challenged him. He felt a quiet warmth at his shoulder instead, as though Dawson stood beside him, watching over him.

"I'm ready to feed it to you," Adam said. "What did you have in mind?"

Jack had closed in behind Kyle, and Carter and Tyler came to stand near Adam. Bailey remained where she was, not looking happy, and Christina stopped serving to listen.

Kyle set his beer on the bar. "I've been thinking about this. You're good at stunt riding. I'm the best of the best at bull riding—I've got a rack of trophies to prove it. If we try to compete in each other's best sport, we'll both lose."

"I don't know," Adam said. "I've watched you fall off plenty of bulls. It doesn't look that hard."

A couple guys, including Jack, chuckled, but Kyle ignored them. "So what I came up with was, a special competition, just for you and me. I set it up with the Fall Festival coordinators and judges— they'll decide what you have to do to prove your best skills, and what I have to do to prove mine. And they and the audience will be the final judges. Sound good?"

"Seems fair," Adam said. He wouldn't put it past Kyle to sweet-talk the judges into doing exactly what he wanted, but Adam couldn't argue, not with the whole bar watching.

"All right then." Kyle stuck out his hand, always having to play the good sport. "May the best man win."

"All right." Adam shook his hand.

"What's the prize?" A woman in a skimpy top asked. She eyed the two with an eager look, as though ready to offer herself to the winner.

Kyle winked at her. "We haven't decided. How about the loser does whatever the winner tells him to?"

Adam shrugged. "Sounds good." He glanced behind Kyle to Bailey, to see how she was reacting to this, but Bailey was gone. *Shit.*

The rest of the bar crowded around them, talking and laughing, starting to take bets. Adam pushed through them, leaving Kyle behind, but Bailey was nowhere in sight.

"I saw her leave," one man said, and grinned. "Don't tell me you lost track of her already, Campbell."

Adam resisted the urge to punch him, thanked him instead, and walked out of the bar.

"You going after Bailey?" Kyle asked behind him.

The night was mild, just right after a hot day, or would be if Kyle weren't following him.

"Yes," Adam said tightly.

Kyle fell into step beside Adam, not trying to stop him, but not dropping away either. "She picked you," Kyle said. "I'm not happy about that, but it's her choice. But I'm just going to tell you, I don't like the way you treat her."

Adam stopped and swung around, forcing Kyle to a halt. "What the hell are you talking about?"

"I'm talking about the way you don't stick with anyone. When Bailey's around you, she looks happy and miserable at the same time—probably because she knows you're a love-em-and-leave-em kind of guy. That's a polite way of saying man-whore. She doesn't need that, especially not right now. She's still hurting, and I don't want to see her hurting more."

"Hurting Bailey isn't at the top of my list," Adam said in a hard voice. "She's the best thing this town will ever see."

"Yeah, you have an answer for everything." The anger in Kyle's eyes was true, and went deeper than his usual rivalry with Adam. "She might not want me for anything serious, but no matter what happens between her and me, Bailey is my *friend*. Always has been. You treat her right, or I will come after you for real. I don't care if you just recovered—I'll break your leg again, *and* your other one, and mess up the side of your face that's still pretty."

Adam took a step back. His heart burned, and for once, he didn't want to come back at Kyle's threats with a few of his own. "If I hurt her," he said. "I'll deserve it."

He gave Kyle a nod, turned, and strode away from him.

**

Bailey opened the door to Adam's knock. He stood under the circle of porch light, the glare brushing his dark hair and not hiding the scars on his face.

He didn't smile, didn't push his way in. He just said, "Hey."

Bailey folded her arms, her throat tight. "Are you and Kyle done shoving each other around the playground?"

Now his sinful grin came. "You know if I backed down from his challenge, he'd never let it go."

"Yes, I know that, but I'm not helping you get on your feet again just to win some stupid bet with Kyle."

"'Course not. But you don't want me to lose, do you?" Adam let his eyes go wide, giving her that innocent and charming look.

Bailey shook her head, but she backed up and waved him into her house. "You'll do what you want. You always do."

Adam didn't answer as he entered but stood looking around the living room. "I like this house. You did good with it. It's homey."

Bailey had furnished the living room with antique store finds, Hill Country being full of such places. She'd gone for the Edwardian look but with modern comforts, and now everything was muted reds, blues, and greens, with plenty of wood tones. "I wanted something cozy after my ultra-sleek apartment in Austin," she said. "That place was upscale, but always a little cold. This house has been great—once I got the plumbing and wiring totally redone. No traffic rocketing by at three in the morning, and my neighbors talk to me."

Bailey closed the door as she spoke, wondering what she should do. She'd had sex with Adam twice now, but she didn't feel as though they'd resolved anything. He'd come here for more — she knew that — but where they would end up, she had no idea.

"I don't have any beer, sorry," she said as Adam wandered around, looking at her few trinkets and books, the photos of family and horses on the wall, including a still from her recent shoot with Grant in New Mexico. "I'm not set up for a lot of company."

"I didn't come here for drinks." Adam turned from the photo of Bailey in a plaid shirt, hair in a braid, riding hell-for-leather on Buster. "I'm sorry about in the bar just now. Kyle brings out the asshole in me."

He smiled at her as she came to him, and he leaned to kiss her. Bailey hated that the touch of his lips made her doubts flee — as though he'd stay and make her happy the rest of her life.

He licked across her lower lip, his eyes closing as he pulled her closer.

Bailey was going to surrender — again. And it was going to be as good as before. Maybe better, if they could snuggle down in bed and stay there all night.

A buzzing and jangling made her start. She breathed out again when she realized it was Adam's phone.

Adam kept his arms around her and made a face. "Why did anyone ever think cell phones were a good idea?"

"You should get it," Bailey said, a bit breathless. "If it's your brothers, they'll be here knocking at the door if they need to find you. They'll have figured out where you've gone."

"That's true." Adam heaved a sigh and plucked the phone out of his back pocket. His scowl turned to an expression of surprise. "It's Mark. I should take this."

Mark, his mentor, the man Adam trusted in all things. "Want me to leave you alone?" Bailey asked.

Adam shook his head as he clicked on the phone and answered. "Hey, Mark. What's up?"

"You sound good." The man's voice came clearly, tinny but loud.

Adam took Bailey's hand and pulled her to the couch with him. He sank down on the crocheted afghans they'd made love on two nights ago, and tugged Bailey to sit next to him. "I feel pretty good. A hell of a lot better, anyway."

"You're about to feel even better. I found a new picture for you. It's a modern Western, from a major player, and they're desperately looking for a stunt coordinator. I said you were the right man. The director really likes your work—you've worked with him before—so he's all for it. They want everyone together for the first meeting in late October. Can I tell them you'll be there?"

# Chapter Seventeen

"Stunt coordinator?" Adam asked, a stunned look on his face.

"Yep," Bailey heard Mark say. "Means you get to tell everyone else how to fall down, but you don't have to do it yourself if you don't want to. I figure this is the perfect way to ease you back into work. I know what happened hit you hard. Didn't want to push you before this, but it's a great opportunity."

"Yeah, it is." Adam squeezed Bailey's hand. "It sure is."

"Is that a yes?"

Adam glanced at Bailey, his eyes unreadable. "Do they need to know tonight? Or can I sleep on it and call you back?"

"Yeah, call me back. Don't take too long though—they're getting anxious to get the contracts out." A pause. "How are you doing, Adam? Really. You all right?"

Adam squeezed Bailey's hand again. "I'm much better. Promise."

"I heard about the lawsuit—they sent me all the shit. Don't you worry about that, Adam. I'll take care of it."

"I understand why Dawson's family is upset," Adam said.

"I know you do, because you're an understanding guy, but we can't let them walk all over you. Dawson's brother and his wife made Dawson's life hell—they can take a little bit of hell back. Like I said, don't you worry about it. You concentrate on getting better and back out here to Los Angeles. I've got a service taking care of your apartment, so everything's right where you left it. Just cleaner."

Adam gave a short laugh. "Thanks."

"You take care now," Mark said. "Talk to you soon."

"Thanks, Mark."

They hung up.

Adam was quiet as he laid the phone on Bailey's coffee table. He turned to her, his gaze pensive. "He offered me—"

"I know." Bailey gave him a nod. "I heard. He was loud."

"Yeah, Mark likes to make sure his voice carries. Stunt coordinator on a major picture. That means I work out every stunt, I'm in charge of the budget, hiring the stuntmen ... everything."

"That doesn't come along every day, does it?" Bailey asked.

"No." Adam shook his head, an excited light in his eyes. "Not to me anyway."

"I think you should do it." Bailey said the words in a rush, afraid she'd keep silent otherwise.

Adam studied her, quieting. "Do you?"

"Yes. Like he said, it's a terrific opportunity. I imagine the money will be good."

"Yeah, Mark is good at money. I'll probably be able to negotiate anything I want."

Bailey rubbed Adam's hand, rough and sunburned from today's workout. "Then you should go."

Again Adam said nothing while he looked at her. Bailey reached up and touched the ruined side of his face, brushing her thumb over his scars.

She loved him so much. But if his life, and his heart, was elsewhere, in his work, she wasn't going to be the one who stood in his way.

If she begged him to stay with her, and he did it to please her, that short-term pleasure would turn into resentment on his part. You couldn't get between a person and his dream, or guilt him into not pursuing it. The dream would always win. You'd try to hold them back, then you'd turn around, and they'd be gone.

"Think on it, Adam," she said softly. "Think good and hard. It's your whole life you're talking about. If you decide to go, I'll drive you to the airport."

Adam's blue eyes were steady, no flickering, no indecision. "You're an amazing woman, Bailey. But I always knew that."

"Yeah, well." Bailey ducked her head as though modest, and she forced a smile. "That's what they all say. Tell you what, though—if you're going to get back into stunts *and* show up Kyle at the Fall Festival, we've got a lot of work to do."

"But not right now," Adam said, his voice going low. He smoothed her hair, turning his face up to his and kissed her, his mouth warm, taking his time.

Bailey didn't fight her surrender. What had she told him? *We have to grab on to what we have, and love the people we love as hard as we can while we still have them.* That's what she'd do with Adam.

At least, this time, they made it to the bedroom.

**\***

*Three weeks later ...*

Three weeks of Bailey working Adam's ass off every day, and then making fine, hot love to him at night.

Adam was surprised some mornings he could walk after their wild times. Baily had amazing energy in the bedroom, but she still remained a sweetheart, kind to everyone she saw and well-liked in return, no matter that the entire town knew Adam spent every night at her house.

Not that Bailey cut him any slack as far as riding was concerned. Adam had to admit that Bailey was turning out to be one of the best trainers he'd ever had. She knew when to push and when to let him ease into it, how to guide him into trickier and trickier stunts, until Adam was almost, but not quite, back to his old confidence.

The *not quite* bugged him as the Fall Festival drew nearer. Adam was never certain when he'd have one of the panic attacks, though they'd backed off, and never happened when he was enjoying himself in Bailey's bed.

The years fell away when he was with her, and they'd laugh, tease each other, and play *Do you remember ... ?* until Adam forgot his troubles. Things would be perfect, he thought, if he could only stay lazy with her and let the world go by.

Bailey, of course, wouldn't let him.

The end of the three weeks found Adam standing near the open arena at the county fairgrounds, wondering what in the hell Kyle was going to make him do to humiliate him in front of everyone they knew.

The MC for the rodeo and horseshow portion of River County's Fall Festival had been the class clown when Adam was in school. Clint's father used to be MC; Clint had taken over when he'd retired. Clint was good at it, though the whole county now had to groan at his bad jokes.

Show classes for the kids under twelve came early in the day. Adam hung out near the rail with Carter as Faith entered the ring on Dodie to compete in a Western trail horse class.

Faith had been practicing and practicing for this, and she had each obstacle down, but Adam sensed Carter tense as soon as his daughter rode into the ring.

"Here's a pretty little lady," Clint's voice came over the system. "Riding another pretty little lady. Let's give it up for Faith Sullivan and Dodie."

Applause came from the small crowd and some shouts of encouragement. Adam clapped hard, but Carter stood unmoving, gaze fixed on Faith.

Faith did look pretty, her brown hair in a tight braid under her straw cowboy hat, her jeans and button-down shirt clean and pressed. She rode well, head up, heels down, seat solid, one hand quiet on the reins, the other relaxed on her thigh. Dodie arched her neck and pricked her ears forward, looking eager.

The trail class was an obstacle course, the rider proving she or he could take the horse through it calmly and quickly, without mistakes. Obstacles included a wooden bridge, a gate, rails arranged in an L-shape the horse had to back through, equally spaced poles to trot over, and whatever else the course designer had decided to use this year.

Faith took Dodie through most of the obstacles without a problem, Dodie backing through the L on dainty feet. If the mare stepped outside the poles as Faith backed her, that was points off. Dodie placed her feet carefully, though, coming nowhere near them. Next, she trotted willingly over the evenly spaced poles without touching them, and walked over the hollow, echoing wooden bridge as though she ate scary bridges for breakfast.

At one point, Faith had to turn Dodie in a three-sixty pivot, the horse staying within the confines of a square. Dodie turned in place, hips almost swaying, looking pleased with herself.

"What a gal," Clint said over the loudspeaker as Dodie completed a perfect circle. "She could spin around all day, like a quarter horse pole dancer. Bet she has the geldings wishing they could have something back."

The crowd booed him. Faith, paying no attention, rode Dodie to the last obstacle, the one Faith had the most trouble with. The gate.

"You can do this, baby," Carter whispered beside Adam. His face was tense, the hand that rested on the railing in front of him, clenched.

"She'll be fine," Adam said quietly.

Carter shot him a look then went back to watching Faith.

The rider, still mounted, had to unlatch the gate, open it, take the horse through, close the gate, and latch it up again, without ever taking her right hand from the top of the gate. Faith often lost hold of it on the turnaround, the horse's big body pushing her away. But if she let go, that would mean major points off her score, which would pretty much guarantee she didn't place.

Carter gripped the rail tighter as Faith slowed to approach the gate, her entire attention on it. She was fine leaning down to unlatch it, and in fact, Dodie helped nudge it open, to the crowd's amusement.

"Dodie wants to get through," Clint boomed. "She's sure her boyfriend lives on the other side."

"Careful," Carter said under his breath. "Like we practiced. Don't rush."

Faith got the gate open, and she and Dodie moved carefully through. Dodie's back end swung around, the momentum tugging at Faith's hand. She leaned down desperately, the tips of her fingers barely brushing the wood.

"Dodie's swishing her hips, ready to go," Clint said. "Doesn't want to wait to shut the gate. Ah, there it goes."

Faith walked her fingers along the top rail until she got a firm hold of it again. She pushed the gate closed, using Dodie's turning body to help her, slid the latch into place, and rode triumphantly away.

Carter breathed out again. Adam laughed and clapped him on the back. "Calm down. She was great."

Carter didn't answer, his attention all for his daughter as Faith rode to exit the ring. When she passed Carter, she grinned down at him.

"Dad, did you see me? I nailed it!"

"Yeah, you did," Carter said. "You're beautiful, baby."

Faith beamed with happiness and rode on out to a wave of applause. Adam scanned the crowd on the bleachers, his gaze resting on Bailey, who stood next to his mom, both of them having come to watch Faith.

Bailey looked so calm, smiling and giving encouraging nods to the young riders she knew, some of whom she'd given lessons to. A teacher proud of her pupils.

She'd certainly taught Adam a lot these last few weeks. Foremost, that she was fearless. Whatever Bailey's life in Austin and her failed marriage had done to her, they hadn't defeated her. If anything, that disappointing life had made her throw off her inhibitions and come into her own.

She was no longer the shy Bailey, hoping to be accepted by the cool kids. She stood upright, radiating beauty and confidence.

She'd given that confidence to Adam, working him hard, not letting him give in to his nerves, or whatever it was that had kept him down. Even though he wasn't sure he was ready to perform today, he'd do it anyway. Win or lose, just getting through the challenge would be a major victory.

The trouble was, it hadn't been Kyle or the festival coordinators, in the end, who'd set up whatever it was Adam would have to do. His brothers had. Grant, Tyler, Carter, and Ross knew what Adam could do, and they'd taken over figuring out something that would test his skills, just as Ray and his sister Grace had set up what Kyle would have to do to win.

When Adam asked his brothers why they were taking sides with him against Kyle, Carter said bluntly that they were sick of the rivalry between the two, and that both of them needed their asses kicked.

Did not make Adam more confident.

He was also not confident about leaving after this weekend, win or lose, for Los Angeles. Mark and Adam had talked almost every day since the initial phone call, going over the details for the upcoming job. Adam felt a stir of both fear and excitement with every call, until he'd hang up the phone and look at Bailey.

Taking the job meant leaving her behind.

Not that Bailey was upset about it. She encouraged him to go at every turn, was training him back to one-hundred percent. Not getting in his way. Not begging him to stay.

Dawson would want Adam to go and not sit around and wallow because he got hurt. *You need to get off your ass,* he'd hear Dawson saying whenever he became discouraged these last weeks. *I never sat around saying, oh poor baby, every time you broke your finger, did I? I got you up and got you going. Right?*

Right.

Adam had come back to Riverbend and left it again many times before, his work consuming him. But this time Adam would be leaving more than the town, his family, his home. Once before, he'd walked away from what he'd started with Bailey, and he didn't want to walk away again.

So here he was. Ready to prove to the world that he wasn't down and out. Ready to blow this town and get back to the gritty hard work and fast-paced life of the glittering city.

Bailey caught his eye and smiled.

He was going to miss that smile—and her eyes, and her body beneath his in the night.

He'd almost asked her to come with him, except she'd told him as they'd worked, that she loved it here and would never dream of leaving again. She'd found her home. Adam had to wonder whether she'd volunteered that information to tell him not to bother asking.

The riders of the trail class were called back to the ring, and the winners were announced. Faith won the blue.

She had tears in her eyes as she rode back out with the ribbon tucked into her belt, patting Dodie and praising her. Carter met the pair when they emerged, helping Faith dismount and catching her in his arms for a proud dad hug.

Bailey was on her feet, shouting for Faith. She was lovely in her jeans and bust-hugging white shirt, her smile flashing in the sunshine.

As Bailey left the bleachers, Adam's attention was pulled to another woman sitting a few rows above Bailey. The woman was watching Faith, couldn't take her eyes from her. She looked vaguely familiar, and Adam narrowed his eyes.

Couldn't be ...

Adam looked quickly at Carter, but Carter was walking away with Faith and Dodie, Bailey and Olivia coming to meet them. When Adam looked back at the bleachers, the woman had gone.

\*\*

Christina was working in a vendor's tent the bar had set up for the event. It was an easy gig—take the coupons that had to be bought with ID at the gate, dispense beer or wine into plastic cups, smile at everyone, and stop anyone underage who tried to get the alcohol. Easy enough, because Christina knew everyone, and the teenagers of River County weren't getting away with anything under her watch today.

It was fine until two tickets hit the booth at a relatively quiet time, and a familiar voice said, "Can I get a couple beers from you?"

Christina rose from the shadows where she'd been hooking up a new keg. Grant stilled, his gaze becoming fixed when he saw her. He must not have known it was her back here.

Looking into the blue eyes she used to see above her in the night, as he'd made deep, sweet love to her, was a hell of a hard thing to do. The broad hand that rested on the table had stroked fire through her, the blunt fingertips had slid inside her to bring her to pleasure.

Wouldn't be so difficult if Grant didn't always look so good. Sunshine danced on his dark hair, bringing out the highlights, and his tanned face held the handsomeness of the Campbell brothers. He filled out his black button-down shirt, part of his costume for his upcoming performance, with solid muscle. He'd put on a string tie and a black hat later, but right now, the top button of his shirt was undone, showing a sliver of chest and dark hair.

No one was behind him, and Christina was the only one in the stall. In the crowd that swarmed the fairgrounds, she and Grant were alone.

She made herself turn away from him, take two plastic cups off the top of the stack, and start a stream of beer into one. "Should you be drinking before your ride?" she asked, her voice light.

"They're not for me."

He shut up, not telling her more. Probably they were for some of the groupies who followed him around, showing up at every performance. Grant was always gracious to them. Now that Grant and Christina weren't together anymore, he likely was more than gracious.

The thought of him smiling at one of those young women, touching her like he'd touched Christina, pushed a big lump into her throat.

She set down one full glass and started on the other. She wouldn't spit in them, she promised herself. She wasn't that petty. Nope, not her.

"How's Ray doing?" Grant asked.

Christina's hand shook on the spigot, but she made herself shrug. "He's fine. No permanent damage." She and Ray hadn't gone out much since the accident, but she wasn't going to tell Grant that she spent most nights home, alone. Missing him.

"Good to hear," Grant said.

They were so formal. Like people who barely knew each other. As though Grant hadn't laughed at her in the darkness, saying *I love you, angel. You make everything bad go away.*

Christina put the second beer onto the counter. She slid the tickets off the table and dropped them into the bucket with the others.

Grant reached into his pocket, pulled out a five between two fingers, and reached with it toward her tip jar.

Christina slammed both hands to the counter. "No. Don't you dare."

Grant looked at her in surprise. "Why the hell not?"

"You put that in there, Grant Campbell, I'll take it out and burn it."

Grant's veil of politeness dropped. *Shattered* was a better word. "Doesn't look like you say that to everyone offering you a tip." He glanced at the jar swimming with ones, fives, and a few twenties. "What's wrong with my money?"

"I don't want it, that's what's wrong with it."

Grant looked Christina up and down, *really* looked at her, instead of holding himself remote, as he usually did these days. He let his gaze rest on her bosom, round and full under the black T-shirt with the bar's logo.

"I get it," he growled. He shoved the five back into his pocket, then withdrew a twenty instead and slammed it into the tip jar before she could stop him. He grabbed the beers and turned abruptly away, sloshing liquid all over the place.

Christina snatched the twenty-dollar bill out of the wide-mouthed jar. The paper was still warm from being in his pocket. Christina swallowed, fetched a lighter from under the counter, held the twenty between her fingertips, and set fire to it.

Grant looked back. He stopped and turned all the way around, a beer in each hand, as he watched Christina burning the money. He stared at her, scowling, then he shook his head and strode away.

Christina's eyes stung from the smoke. She dropped the last bits of the bill to the dirt on the ground before the flame could reach her fingers.

Her eyes were watering, and she angrily swiped at them. Her eyes stung even more when she saw Grant reach two women—buckle-bunnies half falling out of the tightest jeans and halter tops she'd ever seen—hand them the beers, then put one arm around each of them and walk away.

"Damn it." Christina turned her back, stalking out of the tent for another keg. It was a long time before her eyes cleared, and she could see straight again.

# Chapter Eighteen

Bailey showed one of the Campbells' newer horses in a halter class, and the filly did well, winning second place. A filly from another ranch in the county, owned by a family who raised world-champion quarter horses, won first. Didn't matter — that horse would probably come to the Campbells to be trained eventually anyway.

The Fall Festival was the biggest event of the year in River County, with plenty for everyone. The baking tents held delectable treats, games for the kids kept them busy and happy, and there would be dancing later tonight.

Bailey had missed this. When she'd lived in Austin, she'd been working too hard on new rollouts every October to leave even for the weekend. She'd made a lot of money as a programmer, but she'd worked her ass off for it almost twenty-four seven.

Life out here moved a little slower, which was what she needed. Even if Adam wouldn't be a part of it after this, she couldn't leave Riverbend. Not now that she'd found a refuge.

Tyler and Grant did some exhibition stunt riding to an appreciative crowd, Bailey helping out. They did a Wild West gunfight on horseback, Tyler playing the good guy, Grant with a black hat, black shirt, and black jeans, playing the bad guy.

They galloped around each other, Tyler on Bobby; Grant on Buster, nearly brushing as they passed. They did a lot of antics, like jumping to a stand on the saddles, pretending to shoot at each other's balls and leaping out of the way, legs spread, just in time. The crowd loved it.

For the finale, they each jumped from their horse to the other's, trying to knock each other off, and missing completely to end up riding the other's horse. At last, Grant leapt at Tyler, ready to finish off the "good guy," appeared to miscalculate, and ended up sitting backwards behind Tyler, looking astonished. Tyler rocketed out of the ring on Bobby, Grant hanging on for dear life to the cheers of the crowd.

Buster, left alone, ran around the ring by himself, bucking and dancing. Bailey's job was to go in and bring him out.

Buster capered around while the audience laughed. Everyone knew Buster.

Bailey stopped in the middle of the ring and held out her hand, calling softly to him. Buster, who'd practiced this with her, swung around and trotted directly toward her, nuzzling her as she caught his reins to lead him out.

"He knows whose company he prefers," Clint boomed above them. "Who can blame him? She's *gaw*-geous."

Bailey led Buster out, catching up with Tyler and Grant who were dismounting Bobby. Grant bore a scowl that went well with his black hat and painted on villain mustache.

"That was great," Bailey said, then frowned when Grant only glared at her. "You all right?"

"Fine," Grant snapped. Then he seemed to realize who he was talking to and took the edge from his voice. "Sorry, Bailey. I'm fine."

He turned away, but Bailey saw his gaze go straight to the bar's tent outside the riding area. Christina, serving customers, was smiling and talking in her animated way. She didn't look over at Grant, which made his scowl deepen.

*Ah,* Bailey thought. Those two being apart was so wrong. Once Bailey finished putting Adam back together, she'd have to start on her sister and Grant.

**

As the sun went down at the end of the full day, Bailey joined the crowd at the rodeo arena for the last event—the challenge between Kyle and Adam. Lights came on, their white glare replacing the softer glow of sunshine.

The face-off between two of the best riders in Riverbend was drawing business. Bailey knew that under-the-table betting had gone on all over town. No one knew exactly what the two would have to do to win, only that it would be a serious task for their abilities.

Bailey knew some of what Adam would have to face, because the brothers had brought her into the circle last night. She'd mostly just given her opinion, and now she bit her lip, wondering if she'd done right. She could warn him—but that would undo any good she hoped the course would have for him.

Kyle's challenge was first. He and Adam walked together into the ring, stood and faced the crowd, the noise of which rose to a fever pitch. Boots stomped on the metal bleachers, and screams and yelling built into a wall of noise.

Kyle raised his arms, hamming it up. Adam simply stood and regarded them calmly.

The two finally turned to each other and shook hands. The crowd loved that—they'd be good sports—but Bailey noted how firm the shake was, how hard they held it.

They broke apart only when a rodeo clown dashed out and threatened to yank them apart. Kyle and Adam made their bows, each retreating from the arena.

A bellow broke through even the noise of the audience. Bailey looked down at the bull chute, and her eyes widened. That couldn't be ...

A white bull was banging around in the chute, the handlers dodging his horns and hooves. The bull was known as the White Devil, one of the highest scoring bulls on the circuit. No one, but no one had been able to stay on him more than a second or two, not even Kyle and Ray, national champion riders.

She saw Kyle on the fence, staring down at the bull, then at his brother. Ray was grinning, teeth flashing in the dim light.

She couldn't hear Kyle, but his body language told her everything. *Shit, Ray, seriously?*

Ray answering. *If you can do this, you'll be a legend.*

*Sure, that'll make me feel better when I'm in a body cast.* Then a shrug. *Oh, well. What the hell?*

Kyle wouldn't back down, Bailey knew. He might lose fair and square, but he'd never give Adam the satisfaction of refusing to compete.

Kyle nodded to the wranglers, set his hat firmly, and climbed over the chute onto the White Devil.

Someone smooshed in beside Bailey. Christina, tired from working all day, and smelling of barbecue smoke from the line of vending tents, sat down, avidly watching the ring.

"Wasn't going to miss this," she said. "I have a hundred-dollar bet with Ray that Adam will kick ass."

"Ray's not mad you bet against his brother?"

Christina shook her head. "He thinks this is all a big joke. I didn't know he'd arranged for the White Devil. I thought they took that bull out and shot him a long time ago."

Apparently not. As soon as Kyle touched him, the bull rocked around like crazy in the narrow chute, unable to move much. But as soon as he was released … watch out.

Kyle set his hat again, settling his right hand under the rope. He looked pale, but maybe that was just the light.

After a long, tense moment, he gave the nod to open the gate.

The Devil shot out, landing nearly on his chest a second later, his back end rising in the air in a gigantic buck. Down the legs came, like pistons driving into the ground. The Devil rose on his hind legs only long enough to replant his front ones to bring his back end up again.

Higher and higher he rose, and Bailey was sure he'd go all the way over, dragging Kyle with him.

Kyle's hand remained under the rope like a rock, while his other arm rose to keep from touching the bull. But every time the bull came down, Kyle's legs clamped around him again, his balance regained.

The clock above the ring was running. One second passed, then two, then three. The crowd was on its feet, roaring for Kyle.

The sound galvanized the White Devil who added sideways twists and spins to his bucks. He moved so fast he was a flash of white, except for the deadly gray spikes of his horns.

Kyle hung on. His hat flew off, but Kyle's concentration was all on the Devil, his legs in chaps moving with the bull.

The clock kept on—five, six, seven, eight. Kyle passed the requisite time, but he hung on as the crowd went insane. Nine ... ten.

Way more than a record on the White Devil, and longer than most rides at all. A buzzer went off. Kyle kept on a few more seconds, then he let go, allowing the momentum of the next buck to vault him to the ground.

He landed more or less on his feet, sidestepping a little to keep his balance. The Devil ran crazy, twisting and dancing. The clowns and wranglers dashed in to round him up, boiling apart when he charged them.

Kyle got well out of the way, bowing and soaking up the adulation of the crowd.

The White Devil didn't want to leave. He evaded the catchers, running around and around the ring. Kyle joined the chase, and at last, seven guys got the bull pushed into a pen, where he bellowed and kicked until he got bored enough to quiet down.

Kyle received a standing ovation. It had been a brave and wild performance. Kyle stood grinning, waving his retrieved hat, and loving it.

Once Kyle finally walked out, his brother high-fiving him and Grace hugging him on the way, the ring went dark. Clint told the crowd to return in half an hour for Adam's turn. Meanwhile, Adam's team would prep.

Bailey left her seat, and went to help them.

**

Adam had no idea what to expect. Ross, looking unusual in jeans and T-shirt instead of his deputy's uniform, kept him away from the arena while it was being set up, but the sound of hammering both unnerved Adam and made him curious. What the hell were his brothers up to?

At the half hour precisely, Ross checked his watch, then gestured Adam to follow him.

The bleachers were full, people standing on top as well as lining the ring. The whole county had come to see Adam either triumph or fall on his face.

*Great. No pressure.*

When the lights came on, Adam experienced both relief and more nervousness. The crowd broke into a delighted cheer.

His brothers had built Adam an obstacle course utilizing old-West set buildings that they often used in their exhibition shows. The configuration was sparse—a storefront there, a corral over there, an overturned wagon, a water trough, and other things scattered about to suggest a movie set on an old Hollywood Western. In the window of the schoolhouse front at the opposite end stood Faith, wearing a sunbonnet.

Clint's voice came on over the loudspeaker. "A peaceful day in the sunny town of Riverbend a hundred and fifty years ago ... or was it?"

The far gate opened, and in rode Adam's brothers, dressed all in black, black masks on their faces. They wore duster coats and had six-shooters on their belts.

"Can our hero, Adam Campbell, save the damsel in distress? Or will the evil Black-Hat boys take him down?"

Grant whooped. He, Tyler, and Carter started around the ring, their fluid movements menacing. Tyler drew his gun and shot a blank into the air.

*So. They were going to both test his skills and make fun of him at the same time.*

"And just to make things a little more interesting ..." Clint said.

The lights dimmed. Adam heard a whoosh, and suddenly every structure in the arena was outlined by flame. Two flaming hoops lit in the middle of the ring, the bluish gas-fed fire dancing high.

Adam pushed Buster's nose away and glared at Ross. "What the hell? Who decided *fire* was a good idea?"

Ross returned his look without expression. "Grant. Well, Grant ... and Bailey."

*Bailey?*

Adam had ridden through plenty of controlled flames on movie sets, many far more intense than this. He'd stood near explosions that came close to singeing all his hair off, had ridden a motorcycle through giant balls of flame. Didn't matter that a lot of moviemakers these days used CGI to enhance shots, they needed a decent shot in the first place, plus the studios Adam regularly worked with liked to keep things as real-looking as possible.

But that had been before he'd been burned, had vivid memories of his clothes in flames, the heat appalling, and Dawson dead before his eyes.

And *Bailey* had decided this was a good idea?

Of course she had. She'd wanted Adam to face his worst fear. He could imagine Grant agreeing it was a good idea, and taking off with it.

Adam felt the heat that had consumed him, smelled the terrible odor of burning metal and flesh, heard the horrified shouts …

*Aw, come on,* the voice of Dawson sounded in his head. *You're not afraid of a little heat, are you?*

So Dawson had said at the beginning of every stunt, even as he and Adam went carefully over all the safety issues and fallbacks.

*Do it for me,* Dawson went on. *Make me proud, kid.*

"We're starting the clock at 90 seconds," Clint boomed over the loudspeaker. "Can he save the girl in time?"

"I'll get you for this," Adam growled to Ross. His baby brother only grinned, though he did look a bit uneasy.

Adam mounted Buster, the horse for once not offering to bite, kick, swat, or coat Adam with drool. He seemed eager to get on with the fun. Adam settled into the saddle, Ross checking the cinch for him and retightening it. Finally, Ross patted Adam's leg and gave him a thumb's up.

The gate swung open, and Adam rode in. Tyler yelled again, and then his three brothers charged him, fire swirling in their wakes, and started shooting at him.

# Chapter Nineteen

Adam knew exactly how to do a take in a Western movie, how to make it look real, and how to get it done efficiently.

Unfortunately, so did his brothers. They were coming to teach him a lesson.

Adam swerved Buster to miss Tyler riding straight at him, pistol firing. *Make it look good,* Dawson whispered to him, then his voice drifted away and the noise of the arena returned.

This was a show to all the people looming around the ring. What they didn't understand was that to stunt riders, every bit was entirely real.

Tyler shot again. A light beamed from the end of the pistol—if it touched Adam, he'd have to behave as though a true shot had hit him. Carter had come up with that idea a while back, to add more realism to their Wild West shows, for the audience's enjoyment. *Thanks a lot, bro.*

Adam was ducking down behind Buster's left side, still in the saddle but clinging to the horn and pommel, even as Tyler's shot went off. The light winked harmlessly overhead, where Adam's torso had been.

Once Adam was past Tyler, he straightened up, pulled out his own pistol, and shot his brother in the back.

"Ow, that hurts," Clint's voice boomed. "Right between the shoulder blades."

Tyler reacted accordingly. He made a big show of jerking in the saddle, then falling back, going off over the horse's rump, his arms flung out to his sides. Tyler hit the dirt and lay still. His horse, loose, raced around the ring, stirrups flying.

Adam reached the first storefront. He had to ride around that, evading Grant and Carter coming at him on either side, then jump Buster over the high water troughs. His brothers were driving him where they wanted him to go, toward the flaming hoops, and the wagon on its side, burning merrily. Anything to keep him from Faith waiting at the end of the run.

Carter came right at him, his eyes over the mask glittering meaner than any real bandit's ever could. He'd have scared the shit out of lawmen out here a hundred years ago, and some of the bandits too.

Adam counterattacked, urging Buster on. Carter swerved at the last minute, the sudden move forcing Adam to turn straight toward one of the rings of fire.

The other side of the hoop was clear. All Adam had to do was jump through, ride around to Faith, and he was done with this stupid test.

Just jump through fire. That was all.

Buster didn't care, but he picked up Adam's nervousness. The unspookable horse shied as Adam rode him toward the hoop, the whump of flames on the wind unnerving.

*Oh, just do it.* Dawson came back, sounding disgusted now. *Your grandmother could make that jump.*

Another thing Dawson had loved to say.

*For you, buddy,* Adam said silently, his jaw tight.

He gathered himself in, calmed Buster, and dove for the hoop.

It was done so fast, Adam never felt the heat. He was through the fiery hoop and on the other side, galloping up the middle of the ring before he could be afraid.

Bailey wasn't so crazy after all.

Not that his brothers were going to let him off so easy. Both circled around, cutting right in front of him, so he had to back Buster in a rapid flurry of hooves. Buster reared, then came down running.

The brothers shot at Adam, and he ducked right then left to shield himself.

"Ten seconds," Clint said excitedly. "Can he make it?"

Carter swerved to block Adam again, but Adam anticipated and cut Buster to the left. Buster almost rolled with the sharp turn, but it caused Carter to overshoot, his horse charging to the other side of the ring.

Grant decided to show off a little. He leapt to his feet on the saddle, moving in perfect rhythm with Bobby beneath him, both his pistols out.

Adam would have made it. Grant was clowning, opening himself up to Adam's shots, and Carter would take a few seconds to regroup. That was all he needed.

The crowd was roaring, urging him on. Faith jumped up and down on her box behind the window. "Come on, Uncle Adam!" she yelled.

With a giant *bang*, one of the burning hoops exploded. The gas that fed it must have overheated or fire had run back up the line, or something.

All Adam knew is that the giant circle of flame expanded—a bright, hot inferno—and Grant, still standing on Bobby, rode right into it.

Bobby swerved in terror, dashing for the darkness of the edge of the ring, and Grant fell into the heart of the flames.

Everything moved in slow motion. Adam saw Grant fall, tucking himself together for a roll to safety. Behind him, Carter turned, saw, and swung back on his reluctant horse. Tyler came alive, leaping to his feet, all three brothers making for Grant.

Grant hit the ground hard, taking it on his shoulder, but Adam didn't see him come out of the flames. Carter's horse pivoted and tried to bolt, fear of the fireball driving him back. Tyler ran for Grant, but the fire wouldn't let him near. Outside the ring, firemen were coming, led by Ross, but too slow, too slow.

Grant staggered up, his duster on fire. He struggled to throw it off, but flame still clung to him, and he fell to his knees. Carter was off his horse, running, but too far away to reach him.

Adam heard a high-pitched scream at the rail. He saw Christina there, her hands to her face, watching in panic. Beside her was Olivia, frozen in shock.

Bailey was next to them both, her gaze fully on Adam.

Bailey's and Adam's eyes met, locked. Bailey gave him the barest nod.

Buster would run at anything, and run true. Adam pointed him in the direction of the fire, dropped the reins, and rode him hard.

When he came to where Grant had fallen, Adam slid his feet free of the stirrups, flung himself from the saddle, caught his brother, and propelled both of them through the fire and out into the dry dirt beyond.

Grant was limp, half conscious. Adam kept rolling with him, Adam on Grant, then Grant on Adam, then both of them landing side-by-side, Grant facedown.

The deadly flames were off Grant's clothes, but Adam got to his knees and beat the sparks on his brother's back and legs until they were out.

Then he rolled Grant over, frantically checking his vitals. Grant coughed, his chest heaving from the oily smoke.

Adam paused, his hand over his brother's heart. "You all right? Can you hear me?"

Grant nodded, coughing again. "You try to give me mouth-to-mouth," he said, voice raw, "I'll shoot you for real."

Adam collapsed. He put his hands to his face, and Adam, who never allowed himself to cry, let tears of relief leak from his eyes.

Behind him, firefighters were putting out the blazes. The other hoops and the fire around the buildings were dark, someone obviously able to cut off the gas to them, but the first hoop still burned merrily, as did the bales of hay the explosion had reached.

The clock had long since buzzed, signaling the end of Adam's challenge. The crowd was worried, watching, speaking in murmurs.

"Help me up," Grant said. "We gotta show them I'm all right."

"You're not all right," Adam said. "For one thing, half your hair is gone."

"What?" Grant put a shaky hand to his head, but Adam pulled it down by his loose sleeve.

"Don't touch. I'll get you up, and then to an ambulance."

"Fair enough."

Adam climbed to his knees. He got his arms under his brother's and pulled them both to their feet.

So he'd done for years and years, ever since the first day Adam had stood Grant upright on his baby feet and told him he could walk.

The brothers faced the crowd, side by side. Grant took one step away from Adam, and waved.

The cheering was thunderous. Faith had come off her platform and was racing toward them, the sunbonnet gone. Carter intercepted her and swept her into his arms. Tyler halted next to them, panting and panicked, propping up Grant's other side. Ross was there too, leading in the paramedics.

The five of them stood, brothers together, with Faith, while the crowd went on and on in their adulation. Faith waved both hands, secure in her father's embrace.

Bailey was at the rail, smiling hard, a light from above haloing her face. She caught Adam's eye, and her smile widened, just for him.

*I love you*, she mouthed. Or Adam thought she did. Then the paramedics swarmed them, and Adam turned away to take care of Grant.

**

The bar was jumping later that night. The festival shut down at eleven, and would start up again tomorrow. Christina, though she didn't have to work, was there with Bailey and the rest of the regulars.

Adam would leave tomorrow for Los Angeles.

The thought had been swimming at the back of Bailey's mind all day. In spite of the distraction of the festival, the worry over Grant, and her guilt of her part in it, the one thought she was trying to avoid — and wouldn't leave her — was that tomorrow, Adam would be gone.

He came in around midnight, with Grant. A shout went up when the pair entered. From what Bailey had gathered from texts from Adam, Grant had been treated for some second-degree burns and released. She'd supposed he'd go home and recover, but there he was, walking next to Adam and Tyler like nothing had happened.

Grant had lost most of the hair on one side of his head, and he'd obviously shaved back the rest. The buzz cut showed off his handsome face, which had escaped too much damage, and made him look like a bad-ass biker. More than one woman noticed this and kept her gaze on him.

Women's gazes followed Adam too. And Kyle, who was there with Ray, Ray's arm around Christina.

"Bailey." Adam reached her while Grant moved to speak to his adoring public. "Talk to you outside?"

The bar had hired a live band tonight, and they slammed out fast-paced music in the corner. They were good, but no way could anyone have a conversation in here.

"I know what you're going to say," Bailey began as soon as she and Adam were well out into the parking lot. The bar was packed tonight, but they managed to find a relatively calm space beyond the line where drinks could be taken.

"You do?" Adam gave her an unreadable look. "*I* don't even know what I'm going to say. I'm winging it."

"I never meant for Grant to be hurt. It was stupid. I'm sorry."

Adam's brows came together. "What? That wasn't your fault."

"The whole thing with the fire. I encouraged them to do it. I thought it would knock you out of your shakes. I should have known—"

"Bailey." Adam's voice cut through hers. He'd been burned slightly, a welt on his good cheek and one on his neck. "These are my brothers you're talking about. Wasn't a thing you could have said to stop them."

Bailey chewed her lip. He had a point—the original idea had been Grant's. Carter and Tyler had expressed misgivings. Bailey had said that a controlled and safe stunt would get Adam used to doing them again. The brothers had taken that theory and run with it. They'd done plenty of safety checks beforehand, but as Grant had explained to her when she'd first wanted to begin stunt riding, *shit always happens.*

"I'm still sorry," Bailey said.

"So am I. But it's done, and it could have been worse. Grant's in there soaking up the attention."

"Yeah, I saw that," Bailey felt a smile come. Grant was good at turning bad situations to his favor. "In that case, what did you want to talk to me about?"

For answer, Adam stepped to her, pulled her into his arms, and kissed her.

Heat spread from his hands, as though he'd absorbed the fire in the ring and was radiating it back to her. The kiss went on, Adam taking her strength, but lending her his.

When he eased away, Bailey let out a breath. "I'm liking what you have to say."

His answering smile undid her. Charming Adam, coming to her again.

"What I wanted to tell you—straight out—is that I'm not taking the movie job. I'm calling Mark tomorrow and telling him I won't be doing it. I'm staying in Riverbend."

Bailey blinked. She took a step back, breaking his hold, confusion washing through her.

"No," she said. She didn't quite mean to say it. It slipped out. Loudly.

"No?" Adam stopped, amazement in his eyes. "What do you mean, *no?*"

Yes, what did she mean? This was what Bailey wanted, right? For Adam to stay? To give them a chance to be together?

Was that what she *really* wanted? For Adam to give up everything he'd won after years of work? Of putting up with shit and facing impossible situations to turn his talent into a career? Every hard thing he'd done, every injury he'd suffered, had been to earn money to send home to his brothers and mom, helping to make Circle C Ranch and the Campbell's training business the most prosperous in Hill Country.

And Bailey wanted him to give it all up ... so *she'd* feel better?

Bailey drew a breath, forcing out her words. "Seriously, you're going to take all the time I put in to you, getting you back on a horse, working you into fighting shape, and throw it all away? You were awesome tonight—your reflexes better than ever, your instincts amazing. If Grant had been in trouble three weeks ago, you'd have never gotten to him in time, never saved him. You dove at him like it was nothing. You were fearless. I was so proud ..."

She trailed off under Adam's hard stare, her eyes moist. "Not fearless," he said, his voice still rough from the smoke. "I was scared shitless."

Bailey shook her head. "No one knew. You didn't think about running to save your own skin—you went straight to Grant and pulled him out of the way. You can do anything, Adam. You just have to believe it."

His brows drew together. "If you mean I have my confidence back, I do. Mostly. Thanks to you."

Adam in the dark was a heart-melting sight—tall and straight-bodied, the light behind him outlining every tight inch of him. He was even better when he was naked, in her bed, his long, tanned body against her white sheets, his wicked smile lighting up his blue eyes.

She could have him there for always, if she would just shut up.

"If you're still afraid, we can keep training," Bailey said. "You go out to California tomorrow, sign the contracts, let them tell you what they need, then come back, and we'll work out the stunts. Me, you, and your brothers. You can do this."

Adam's frown deepened. "Bailey, I keep trying to tell you—I don't want to work on the movie. I want to stay here, help my brothers train horses, maybe go with them on some of the smaller shoots. Find my own place."

"I heard you. I just don't understand *why*." Bailey waved her hands to emphasize her points. "It's a fabulous opportunity. A stunt coordinator. You could make your name. Maybe even move to overall director. Start making your own films. We'll all come to the Academy Awards when you win." She tried to smile, but it died under his flat gaze.

"Hold on ... Hold on." Adam reached for her flailing hands, but Bailey backed a step. "I don't even know if this movie is a sure thing," he said. "They might talk to me and decide they don't want me after all. There's no guarantee in this business." He let out a brief sigh. "That's another reason I don't want to go back. It's too uncertain, too full of greedy people who don't give a rat's ass about anyone—including making a stunt safe enough so the stuntmen don't get killed. I'm never going to forgive them for that. Let Dawson's brother sue them all he wants."

"But that's why you *should* go. The business needs people like you to remind them that stuntmen aren't fodder, easily replaced; that they need to be taken care of. You can make sure *your* guys are safe, that accidents like what happened to Dawson don't happen again."

Adam's frown lessened. He hadn't thought of that, she could see.

"You go," Bailey said. She made a pushing motion at him. "Do what you were meant to do. I didn't help you out all those years ago for you to stay home, and I didn't do it for that this time, either."

She tried to walk around him, to head back for the bar and the celebration inside, but Adam seized her and hauled her back.

"Bailey." His grip was strong, fingers biting down. "Maybe I'm wanting to stay home so bad because of you. I keep hearing how much you love it here, how much you're glad you came back to Riverbend. I know you'll never leave. So I want to stay—where you are."

Happiness flooded her, as did guilt and more confusion. Bailey had spent a year trying to deal with hard emotions, and had finally figured out how to push them away so they wouldn't make her sick or keep her awake at night.

But she couldn't handle them right now. "What I want—what I want most of anything in this world— is for you to be happy." Bailey put her hand on Adam's chest, feeling his heart pounding crazily under her fingertips. "Go," she said softly. "Be happy, Adam."

While Adam stared at her numbly, Bailey broke away, evading his grasp this time. She hurried back to the bar, where her confusion could be swallowed by the jangle of the band and the people there. Her family, her friends, everyone important to her were inside. Adam would go, and that would be that.

# Chapter Twenty

"You know," Kyle Malory's voice came from behind Adam. "You two should get married. You already act married. Can't be together five minutes without having an argument."

Adam swung around to see Kyle blocking his way to the bar, his hat shading his face from the parking lot's lights.

Bailey had already disappeared into the bar. She hadn't understood what Adam was trying to tell her, probably because he hadn't told it right. He wasn't gifted with words. Bailey had this crazy idea that she was holding him back, when she was the one who got Adam going every morning. No way in hell was he going to throw that away.

"I'd think you'd want us to fight," he said to Kyle. "Then you can step in and save her from me."

"Nope. Don't get me wrong. I like Bailey. I *really* like her. She's turned into one hot woman. But as much as I hate losing to you, I know that tricking her away from you wouldn't be a win for me. You two work. Believe it or not, I know when to bow out."

"You won our challenge today," Adam said. "I didn't finish."

Kyle shook his head. "I didn't win. There was an accident. Didn't count. We can have a do-over any time you want." He paused. "But I'm not getting up on that bull again anytime soon. Ray's going to get my boot up his ass over that. Scared the living crap out of me."

"Is that what was all over your pants?" Adam asked, his sense of humor returning. "You did good, though, much as I hate to admit it. Anyone else would have called off the bet and gone running for the hills."

"I almost did when I saw what was waiting in that chute for me. But, hell, I did it." A grin lit Kyle's face. "Set a record for riding the un-ridable bull. I am pretty good, aren't I?"

"Don't push it, shithead."

"Tell you what, though," Kyle said. "It'll make every other bull I ride seem like a kitten in comparison. I'll win every championship until I retire. So, thank you."

"Yeah, you're terrific. Don't get a big head."

Kyle chuckled. "You always bring out the worst in me, Campbell. And the best. You know, I think I've done as well as I have in my life because I refuse to be showed up by you."

Adam knew damn well the same thing could be said in reverse. Not that he'd tell Kyle that. "You can thank me then," he said.

"Yeah, you've always been an arrogant shit." Kyle pushed his hat to the back of his head. "Ross told me about your friend getting killed. I'm sorry. That sucks."

Adam clamped his lips together and gave him a nod. "Thanks."

"I know when I got the news that my brother was in the hospital, maybe dying because of that stupid wreck, it was like my world dropped out from under me. He pulled through with only a few scratches, but I sure hated it when I didn't know what was going to happen to him. And this is *Ray* we're talking about. My shithead big brother who decided I should ride the White Devil."

"I'm glad he wasn't hurt," Adam said, meaning it.

"Me too. Just don't tell him."

Adam's grin broke through his tightness. "He'll never hear it from me."

"Good. Now, what are you going to do about Bailey?" Kyle looked him up and down. "She's a fine woman. One of the best. Are you going to let her go?"

"Hell, no."

"Then get in there and go after her. There's plenty of guys in that bar who'll jump on her the second they think she's available. Do I have to make you do everything?"

"Shut the hell up, Malory," Adam said. Kyle was right, but only to a point. "Come on inside with me. Watch and learn."

Kyle snorted a laugh. "This I gotta see."

The bar inside was still in chaos. The band was grinding out a song and couples were spinning to the fast beat. When Adam walked in, he saw Christina approaching Grant. Whatever she said to him was lost in the noise, but Adam came close enough to hear Grant's answer. "You're with Ray," he said in a hard voice, then turned and walked away.

Christina watched him go, her broken heart plain to see. She started to head for the door, but Adam stopped her.

"Stay," he said in her ear, making his voice as gentle as he could under the circumstances. "I need you to. I want you to hear this."

Christina looked puzzled, then as she got a good look at his face, interested.

Adam moved from her and headed up to the band. No way would Bailey be able to make out what he was saying in this racket, and she wasn't about to leave the bar with him again. He had no choice.

As the song ended, and everyone screamed for more, Adam stepped up to the lead singer and spoke into his ear.

"Sure, man," the singer said with beer-scented breath, and handed him the microphone.

"Hey, y'all," Adam said into the mike. "Listen up." His voice boomed across the room, and one of the techs winced and adjusted something on a board. The crowd turned, sending up a cheer for Adam. The cheer was slurred—they were partying pretty hard tonight.

"I just want to thank y'all for helping my brother out," Adam said. "Today, Grant Campbell proved he can fall on his ass and catch himself on fire at the same time. He appreciates your support."

Laughter. Shouting and stomping. Grant gave Adam the finger and a grin.

"I also appreciate something," Adam went on. He had no idea what he was going to say—only that he had to say it, and if he stopped to choose his words, he'd never get through this. "I appreciate a lady here who, when I fell on *my* ass, picked me up, dusted me off, and gave me the push to get going again. She's right over there. Her name is Bailey Farrell."

Cheers. More clapping and stomping. Tyler yelling, "Yeah, Bai-*lee*."

Bailey stared at him in shock. A little space cleared between her and Adam, she in a tight shirt with lace at the neckline, her jeans hugging her hips. Her lips were parted, her beautiful eyes on Adam.

Adam continued, his gaze only for Bailey. "So what I have to say to you, Bailey, is …" And he ran out of words. He never knew what things women liked to hear anyway. All he had to do was smile, but that didn't always work with Bailey.

He tried again. "What I have to say to you is … I love you."

A few *Awws* went through the crowd. A swallow moved down Bailey's throat, her eyes enormous.

"The other thing I want to say to you is … Bailey Farrell—will you marry me?"

The crowd dropped into stunned silence. Then the cheers began again, and the people of Riverbend started weighing in. "Go for it, honey!" "Don't do it, Bailey; save yourself!" "Damn, Campbell, you got balls."

Adam ignored them all. He looked only at Bailey, who watched him in return, her chest rising with her agitated breath.

When she didn't answer, Adam's heart began to sink. She was going to refuse, walk away, be angry with him for embarrassing her.

Didn't matter. Adam would go after her. Again and again, as long as he could, asking her over and over until her *no* became a *yes*. He could roam the country making stupid movies, or he could stay here and keep his brothers out of trouble. Either way didn't matter—as long as Bailey was in his life.

Adam took a breath to tell her it was all right, she didn't have to answer right away, when Bailey gave him a dazzling smile and shouted,

"Yes!"

The noise in the bar was deafening. Somehow Adam got rid of the microphone, somehow he got off the little stage and to Bailey. Maybe he flew—he didn't know.

He grabbed Bailey in his arms and spun around with her, once, twice, three times, lifting her high before setting her down and sinking into the best kiss of his life.

Around them, his brothers and friends were laughing, shouting, going crazy with noise. Adam heard nothing but Bailey's *yes*, felt nothing but her body in his arms, her lips on his.

"Love you," he said.

"Love you too, Adam," she yelled over the racket. "I love you too!"

She pulled him down to her, crying, his sweet Bailey, his anchor in the world's storms.

The band started playing again, the classic, "I Can't Stop Loving You." Everyone around them found partners, pulling each other close, surrounding Adam and Bailey in the middle of the floor.

"Wait," Bailey said to Adam. She reached up with her thumb to wipe tears from his eyes. "What about your movie? We haven't finished *that* fight."

Adam leaned down to speak into her ear. "Nope. Because you're coming with me."

"What?"

"I said, you're—"

"I heard what you said. I meant, what are you talking about?"

"I'll need a wrangler for the horses. You've proved to be a terrific one—look at what you can do with Buster. Since I get to hire my own crew, I pick you. We'll go together, make that movie, and come on home."

Bailey stared at him, joy and astonishment in her eyes. "Seriously?"

"Seriously."

"You want *me* to work on a major movie with you?"

"Yep," Adam pulled her close again. "I just said so."

"You are awesome, Adam Campbell." Bailey burst out laughing. "How do you know what makes me happy?"

He gave her a mock frown. "Wait, are you happier about the movie or marrying me?"

Bailey slanted him a mischievous look, and he knew he was in for a lifetime of her teasing the hell out of him.

"Which do *you* think?" she asked.

"I don't care," Adam said, deciding. "As long as you're with me, I don't care."

"I love you," Bailey said. She rose on tiptoes, gave his earlobe a bite, and said, "Now how about we ditch this place?"

"Hell, yeah."

Adam led her out. Or tried to. They were swamped by his brothers and Christina, all trying to crush Bailey in smothering hugs.

It would always be like that, Adam knew. He'd want Bailey all to himself, but his mom and brothers would be there, and her sister, plus Adam's cute-as-a-button niece, and all their friends, wanting Bailey's attention. The whole damn town, really, because no one in Riverbend could mind their own effing business.

As he and Bailey walked out, hand-in-hand, followed by yells of congratulations coupled with indecent suggestions, Adam knew that all that was fine with him.

Bailey said it best when she opened the door to her house not far away, and turned on the doorstep to kiss him.

That kiss led to a deeper one, which led to Adam sliding his hands under her shirt to cup her soft, hot-as-summer skin. And *that* made Adam push her inside before he ended up undressing her on her tiny front porch.

"Come on in," Bailey said, giving him a wink that made his blood sear. "You're home now."

She took his hand and led him inside, shutting out the night, then to her bedroom, where they found each other once more, and didn't let each other go until morning.

**End**

# Note from the Author

Welcome to Riverbend! I'm thrilled to introduce the Campbell family and their rivals, the Malorys, in the small ranching town of Riverbend, in Texas Hill Country.

Though I have written many romance novels, mostly historicals and paranormals, this is my first foray into contemporary romance. While it's strange for me not to write about men who turn into wolves, wildcats, or bears, or who aren't Scottish lairds, I have long been wanting to write contemporary stories, particularly about this family, who have been living in my head for a while now.

There will be books for each of the brothers – the next one in line is Grant, and then Carter, going down from oldest to youngest. You'll also learn more about the Malory brothers, Kyle and Ray, and their sisters, Grace and Lucy, and more about Carter's past and his daughter, Faith.

I hope you enjoyed the first look at the Campbells and their friends and family. Thanks for reading!

As a bonus, I've included a sneak peek at Grant's story, plus a recipe for Mrs. Ward's harvest pie that Bailey and the Campbells enjoyed. I hope you like it too!

For more information about my books, current and forthcoming, in all my series, see my website, www.jenniferashley.com While you're there, sign up to my newsletter to stay informed about books as they are released.

*Jennifer Ashley*

Please continue for a preview of

*Riding Hard: Grant*

Book 2
of the

Riding Hard series

by

Jennifer Ashley

# Grant

## Chapter One

He wasn't supposed to be here.

Christina slid beers to two customers in the bar Friday night, barely paying attention when they told her to keep the change. She didn't notice anything—not the hot, swirling air, thumping music, the loud talking and laughing of the patrons.

Grant Campbell had just walked in.

Not alone. Grant was never alone. If he wasn't with his brothers, he had women with him, usually more than one.

Tonight, it was three. Two wore their hair long; one had cropped it short and cute. All three wore jeans that might slide from their slim hips any second, tops that were so tight they might have been painted on.

They were beautiful, of course, in that blond, smooth-faced Texas way. Why was it that every woman who followed Grant around was a walking cliché?

Except Christina, of course. She had black hair that curled and would never lie straight, a body with more cushioning than she liked, and her dad's nose. *You're a Farrell, honey,* her dad liked to say. *No denying it.* He said it proudly, because he loved her, but Christine had long ago realized she'd never be petite.

The girls with Grant were shrimpy. Skinny, except for breasts that couldn't be real. No woman was a perfect right angle like that.

The young women hung on him, fighting for which two would have his arms around them. Grant was grinning, the idiot, loving the attention.

Other men shouted hello to him or gave him looks of envy. But of course, Grant was a trick rider and a movie stuntman, which was near enough to movie star for the folks of River County.

Grant got the buckle bunnies to settle down at a table, while he turned to approach the bar.

He stopped between one beat and the next, his blue eyes stilling as his gaze fell on Christina. He hadn't realized she'd be here tonight.

Then he came on. Grant didn't lose his smile, didn't look the least apologetic. He was well-loved in Riverbend, this was Friday night, and this was Riverbend's only bar. He had every right to be there.

Christina could have turned aside and let the other bartender wait on him. She could have slipped out to the tables she was watching, pretending she never saw him. Instead, she made herself step to the bar and give him a neutral look.

"Hey, Grant. What can I get you?"

His eyes flickered. Christina would not— *absolutely would not*— think about how he'd used her polite inquiry the first time he'd walked in here when he'd been twenty-one to get her to go out with him.

*What can I get you?*

*You,* he'd said with a grin. *Or your phone number. Or you meeting me at the coffee shop tomorrow.*

Christina got propositioned every night, often in similar phrases. But Grant had turned on his Campbell charm, his beautiful blue eyes warm, and Christina had found herself falling for him.

She'd known Grant and his brothers most of her life. She'd gone to school with him, but he was three years younger than she was, and when they'd been kids, she'd barely noticed him.

In the time between high school and his first legal entrance into the bar in Riverbend, he'd sure grown up. He'd become tall, deep-voiced, and hard-muscled, tough from all the riding and stunt work he did.

In the years following, while Grant and Christina had dated, then moved in together, Grant had grown up even more. Now he was a hot, hard-bodied man, successful, handsome, well-off . . . And he still had that kick-ass grin that had every woman in the county falling at his feet.

The frozen moment passed. Grant pretended to relax. "Four beers. Whatever's on tap tonight. Oh, make one of them a light beer."

"Watching your weight?" Christina asked as she lifted four mugs between her fingers, arranged them in front of her, and positioned the first one under the tap.

Grant decided not to answer. "What are you doing here tonight?" he asked. "Thought it was Bailey's bachelorette party. Male strippers, and everything." He didn't meet her gaze when he said *male strippers*.

"Starts later. I came in to help out a little." Christina thumped one beer to the bar, swiftly wiping up the foam that spilled out. "What about you? It's Adam's bachelor party tonight too."

Grant shrugged. "Heading there. My friends got thirsty."

Christina didn't reply, especially since one of his "friends" now sauntered up to the bar to lean beside him. She was the short-haired one, and had big green eyes framed with so much mascara Christina was surprise her eyelids didn't gum together.

"We're always thirsty," the young woman said, giving Christina a confident smile. "Keeping up with Grant is exhausting."

Grant's and Christina's gazes met. Christina saw Grant's eyes soften and stop short of rolling. He knew the girl was a bubblehead, and he knew Christina knew it too.

Christina and Grant shared a tiny moment, the two of them connected, the deep friendship they'd formed long ago showing itself for a brief space of time.

The glass at the tap overflowed, and the moment broke. Christina snapped the handle up, poured out the excess foam, and shook the beer off her hand.

"That's one light, right?" she said as she thunked the glass to the bar and moved the next glass under the light beer tap.

"For me," the short-haired girl said. "I'm trying to lose twenty pounds. I've already lost six."

She waited for Christina's praise. Christina swept her a critical look, and decided that if the woman lost even *one* more pound, she'd be skeletal.

"Good for you," Christina said without inflection.

Grant said nothing. She remembered when he'd once said, *I don't like skinny women. You never know when something sharp is going to jam you in the eye.*

He caught Christina's gaze, and another flicker passed between them.

Christina set the third mug on the bar. Grant grabbed that one and another and shoved them into the girl's hands. "You take those back for me, sweetheart," he said. "I'll be right there."

The young woman gave him a sly look. "Better hurry." She shot him a wide smile, then sashayed away, raising the glasses at her friends.

"You taking them with you to Adam's party?" Christina asked as she filled the last mug. "Are they old enough? I should card them."

"You know me better than that, Christina," Grant said, losing his smile. "At least, you should."

"No." Christina finished the last beer and thumped the mug to the bar. She printed out his bill and set it next to him. "I don't think I ever did know you."

Grants brows slammed together. He pulled his wallet from his back pocket and yanked out a couple of twenties. "Keep the change," he said.

"No." Christina swept up the bills. "I told you before, I don't want tips from you."

Grant stilled. Last fall at the rodeo grounds, Christina had worked a booth serving drinks. When Grant had bought some beer then tried to drop a twenty into her tip jar, Christina had yanked out the money and burned it.

Grant's gaze met Christina's again, anger sparking deep in his blue eyes sparking. "Just keep it," he snapped, then he grabbed the last beer and walked away.

Christina pretended not to watch his very fine ass as she counted out the change and slapped it back on the bar. Pretended, but she couldn't take her eyes off him. Grant was tall, broad-shouldered, every part of him good—back *or* front. *Damn it.*

She swung around, grabbed dirty glasses from the other side of the bar, and started furiously washing them.

When she turned back, it was to see Grant sitting at the little table with all three women half on his lap, the four of them laughing like maniacs.

*Shit.*

"Hey, you've got a tip here," a deep voice rumbled at her. Ray Malory's tall body blocked Grant and his sweeties, his hard face softened with a look of welcome.

"Yeah." Christina felt a frisson of relief. She ignored the money and rested her arms on the bar, sending Ray a smile. "Haven't seen you in a while."

"Just got back. Championships in Lubbock this week. I told you about that."

"Oh, I know. It just seemed like a long time."

Ray liked that. He gave her a warm look with his green eyes. "If I'd known you missed me so bad, I would have tried to come home sooner."

Christina laughed. "No, you wouldn't. The day you leave a rodeo early is the day you're done."

Ray had to grin. "How about a beer to celebrate? Hurry it up, barmaid. I tell you, the service in this place is terrible."

"You're a shit." Christina felt a little better as she turned to pour him a beer. At least somebody was interested in talking to her. She didn't have to giggle and jiggle to catch Ray's attention.

The warmth that began vanished as soon as she turned to see Grant throw his head back and laugh.

Christina loved the way Grant laughed. He opened himself all the way, no holding back. He was a warm-hearted man, liking everyone, wanting the world to like him. Not a mean bone in him.

Yet, he could fight with the best of them. His arguments with Christina had been loud, long, and passionate. The making up afterward had been just as passionate.

One of the young women managed to plant herself all the way on his lap, take his face in her hands, and kiss him on the mouth.

The bottom dropped out of Christina's world. She set the beer down, and Ray said something to her, but she couldn't hear. She could only see the young woman with short hair kissing Grant, and Grant's big hands coming around her waist, holding her steady, just as he'd held Christina for so long, never letting her fall.

"*Christina.*"

Christina dragged her attention back to Ray, who wasn't smiling anymore. He turned his head to follow Christina's line of sight, then looked at her again, his mouth a grim line.

"Why don't you call me when you're over it?" Ray shoved a bill onto the bar—way over-tipping, as Grant had—and got himself off the barstool.

Christina's heart squeezed with remorse. "Aw, come on, Ray. Wait."

"Listen, baby, I don't need to worry about who you're thinking about when you're with me. You give me a call when you decide." Ray swept up his beer and walked away, raising his hand to friends across the room.

"Damn it." Christina forced herself not to look at Grant, but the double-kick of Ray walking away had her gut clenching.

Ray was a good guy—he didn't deserve to be hurt. He was also very attractive, with his dark hair and sinful green eyes.

But in the end, he wasn't Grant. He'd never be what Grant had been to her, and Ray knew it. *Damn, damn, damn.*

"You need to go," the other bartender, Rosie, said to her. Rosie's eyes twinkled. "Your sister's party, remember? Go—have fun. I got it."

"Thanks, Rosie. Here." Christina gave Rosie the tab and money Ray had left. "Keep the tip for yourself. I gotta go."

Christina signed herself out on the computer, gave Rosie a brief hug, and took up the change she'd slapped on the bar for Grant.

On her way out, she stopped at Grant's table. The short-haired woman, still on Grant's lap, looked triumphant, but the other two were waiting to cut her out. Grant looked indifferent—if Christina and the rest of the world wanted to watch him with other women, it was their problem.

"You left your change," Christina said to him. She dropped it on the table between the drinks. "Y'all have a good night."

She walked away. If she swayed her butt a little on purpose, gaining the attention of every male in the place, who cared?

Grant sure didn't. Christina's heart ached, but she made herself walk away. They were done, had been done, and there was nothing more to it. She had to get on with her life.

No matter how freaking hard that was going to be.

### End of Excerpt

# Mrs. Ward's Harvest Apple Pie

Harvest pies can vary depending on the season, from just apples, to apples and nuts, to a mixture of nuts, to pumpkin/squash and sweet potatoes, or a mixture of any of the above. This pie brings together juicy apples and the crunch of pecans. If you prefer a different nut, try walnuts or toasted almonds.

**Makes one 9- or 10-inch pie**

**Ingredients**

**Apples**: Six to eight medium to large apples (**Note:** tart ones such as Granny Smith are best, but use your favorites or what you can easily find. I used Washington Braeburn in one pie as I tested this recipe, and it was incredibly delicious! A mixture of apple types works well too.)

Juice of one lemon

Brown sugar: 1 cup

Flour: 4 Tbsp

Cinnamon: 1 1/2 tsp

Nutmeg: 1/2 tsp

Cloves: 1/4 tsp (optional)

Pinch of salt (say 1/4 tsp)

Butter: 2 Tbsp

Vanilla: 1/2 tsp

Chopped pecans (about 1/2 cup or as many as you like), or pecan halves

Additional all-purpose flour for flouring board and rolling pin

To finish:

Butter: 1 Tbsp, melted

Cinnamon sugar (one part cinnamon to one part sugar—you can make a lot of this, shake it up in a jar, and keep to sprinkle on toast or ice cream)

### Crust

This pie uses two crusts—one bottom, one top. Crusts can be store-bought (refrigerated or frozen), or homemade (see **Homemade Crust** instructions below). If frozen, thaw and keep in refrigerator as you prepare the apple mixture.

### Equipment

Pie pan, 9 or 10 inch

### For filling:

One large glass bowl, one small bowl (of any type)

Saucepan (large, heavy-bottomed)

Measuring cups and spoons

Large spoon for mixing

### For homemade crust:

One large glass or stainless steel bowl

Pastry blender (substitute two table knives or forks, or fork and knife)

Marble bread board (or clean and lightly floured counter top) **Note:** marble or counter top keeps pie dough cool as it's worked.

Rolling pin

### Instructions for Filling

1. Squeeze juice from lemon into large glass bowl.

2. Peel and core apples. Slice into thin (approx 1/8 inch) slices and toss with lemon juice in the big bowl as you go.

3. In a separate bowl, mix brown sugar, flour, cinnamon, nutmeg, optional cloves, and salt.

4. Melt 2 Tbsp butter in a large, heavy saucepan. Add apples and turn to coat.

5. Add sugar/flour mixture and vanilla and toss with apples in the pan to coat. Sauté apple mixture in the pan for another 2 minutes on medium low heat. Remove from heat and let cool.

6. **For homemade crust only:** As apple mixture cools, divide pie dough in half (refrigerating one half for top crust). Using floured rolling pin, roll out bottom pie crust on a lightly floured marble board or lightly floured counter, working quickly — roll in one direction, turn dough, roll in one direction, etc.

7. Once dough is rolled out into a large, thin circle, fold crust loosely in half, then in half again. Lift dough to middle of pie pan, and unfold.

Press crust lightly into pie pan—roll rolling pin across the top of the pan to cut off excess crust.

8. **For all crusts:** Prick crust all over with a fork and set in the refrigerator for at least 20 minutes.

9. Preheat oven to 350 F. Set oven rack to lower third of oven.

10. Remove crust from refrigerator (homemade or store bought). Spoon in apple mixture, spreading evenly.

11. Sprinkle 1/2 cup chopped pecans (or more to taste) over the apples. If using pecan halves, lay as many as you want over the top of the apples.

12. Roll out second crust and lay over apple mixture in pie pan. Crimp edges to seal (press them lightly together). Make slashes in the top crust so steam can escape.

13. Brush top crust with melted butter and sprinkle cinnamon sugar over crust.

14. Bake in a pre-heated 350 oven for 45-50 minutes. Pie is done when top crust is golden brown and apple juices bubble from the top.

15. Remove from oven and cool on a wire cooling rack.

Pie is good served warm, and equally good cold the second day, when flavors have melded.

## Homemade Crust

Pie crust is tricky, but I've had very good results from mixing two parts all-purpose flour with one part cake flour.

For two crusts (top and bottom)

1 cup all-purpose flour + 1/2 cup cake flour

1 Tbsp sugar

12 Tbsp butter (1 1/2 sticks)

2 Tbsp shortening (optional — **Note:** If not using shortening, add another 1 Tbsp of butter)

1/2 cup of ice-cold water (measure out 1/2 cup of water and add ice to it)

Pinch of salt

Additional all-purpose flour for flouring board

1. Mix together flours, sugar, and salt

2. Slice butter into small cubes with a table knife, working quickly. If butter warms or gets slick during the process, place it back into refrigerator to cool a few minutes before proceeding.

3. Add cut-up butter and 2 Tbsp of shortening, if using, to flour mixture.

4. Using a pastry blender or two knives or forks, cut cubes of butter plus shortening the into flour mixture until the butter and flour are coarsely blended. The mixture should look like small peas, and a pinch should just hold together.

5. While stirring mixture with a fork, add most of the ice water (not the ice). Mix until the dough just holds together. If too wet, add flour, a tablespoon at a time, and mix. If too dry, add dribbles of water.

6. Dough should just come together when squeezed in your hand, but not be too gooey or too dry and ragged.

7. Working quickly, turn dough out onto clean, lightly floured counter or lightly floured marble board. Press the dough across the board with your hand to incorporate any loose pieces, then gather into a ball.

8. Flatten dough into small disk with your hands, place into a plastic bag (gallon zip-closure bags work nicely), and put into the refrigerator.

9. Let the dough chill at least 30 minutes before using. Proceed to #6 in Instructions for Filling, above.

**Enjoy!**

# About the Author

*New York Times* bestselling and award-winning author Jennifer Ashley has written more than 75 published novels and novellas in romance, urban fantasy, and mystery under the names Jennifer Ashley, Allyson James, and Ashley Gardner. Her books have been nominated for and won Romance Writers of America's RITA (given for the best romance novels and novellas of the year), several *RT BookReviews* Reviewers Choice awards (including Best Urban Fantasy, Best Historical Mystery, and Career Achievement in Historical Romance), and Prism awards for her paranormal romances. Jennifer's books have been translated into more than a dozen languages and have earned starred reviews in *Booklist*.

More about Jennifer's books and series can be found at www.jenniferashley.com

Or email Jennifer at jenniferashley@cox.net

Made in the USA
Lexington, KY
31 March 2015